Sancha reached to a small hearth in the wall at her side and took an iron rod from a bed of coals. The tip glowed cherry-pink. She looked at it a moment, then pressed it to the skin of Sallee's left buttock. Sallee shrieked.

Sancha smiled. "She sings nicely, doesn't she? You wouldn't believe the song she sang for me, Raider, *querido*. Perhaps you'll sing for us too—Mr. Pinkerton Detective."

"I'll see you fry first," he gritted.

Sancha laughed. "Oh no. Sallee perhaps. Maybe you as well—certain parts of you, *¿comprende?*" She jerked her head. "Strip him and hang him up."

THE FIREBRANDS

BERKLEY BOOKS, NEW YORK

To Joan Marie

THE FIREBRANDS

A Berkley Book / published by arrangement with
the author

PRINTING HISTORY
Berkley edition / October 1983

ISBN: 0-425-06380-1

A BERKLEY BOOK® TM 757,375
Berkley Books are published by The Berkley Publishing Group,
200 Madison Avenue, New York, N.Y., 10016.
The name ''BERKLEY'' and the stylized ''B'' with design are
trademarks belonging to Berkley Publishing Corporation.

PRINTED IN THE UNITED STATES OF AMERICA

CHAPTER ONE

"Gentlemen," the tall red-bearded man said slowly, leaning forward and bracing himself on the table with his long gangly arms, "the situation has become intolerable."

The three men seated on the benches of the table in the center of the common room of Hugo's Roadhouse looked at him. On his right sat a stout man in a blue three-piece suit pin-striped in black; he had a double chin and wide blue eyes, and his mouth was totally obscured by a sweeping blond mustache. He had a napkin tucked into his stand-up collar and was gnawing busily at the chicken the innkeeper's wife, a gaunt hollow-eyed woman with black hair drawn back in a severe bun, had just placed before him on a blue-rimmed china plate. Beside him a slim man whose black frock coat and tie contrasted with the plump red pudginess of his clean-shaven face sat with arms folded across his chest, crossing and uncrossing his legs. Across from the man in the black coat was a tall wiry man with jet-black hair and mustache, and with piercing dark eyes set in a face cured like old leather by sun and wind. He was hunched over a tankard of lager beer, clutching it as if he meant to leave fingerprints in the pewter handle. All three were intent on the tall man, each in his own way displaying tight-wound tension by his posture.

The innkeeper bustled in with a tankard and a glass of soda pop on a tray. "Vhen vill Mr. Silver be here?" he asked. He set the mug down in front of the red-bearded man and placed the soda before the man in the black coat.

The stout man laid down his roast chicken and dabbed at his lips with his napkin. "Yes, Wilson, what could be keeping Silver? Surely we can't discuss . . . things without him."

"He's an elderly gentleman, Frank," said the man at his side, "Perhaps he's fallen ill."

The lean party across from him drained his tankard, his prominent Adam's apple riding up and down, then slammed the mug down before him. "Damned if I care what's happened to some old Jew. Let's git started."

The fat man blinked. He had unusually long eyelashes for a man, silky and pale. "That's no way to talk, Jim. Benjamin has been very helpful."

The bearded man cleared his throat. He was a lawyer and a good one, and recognized the time for some of his best courtroom manner. "The matters at hand will not wait, gentlemen, no matter whether we will or will not." He straightened and grasped his lapels with both hands. The knuckles were large, furred with hair like fine copper wire. "I propose that we begin."

"Somethin's gotta be done!" The lean man stared from beneath his wild shock of hair as if daring someone to disagree. "This bastard Durán's bleedin' us white!"

"But what can we do, Mr. Odelbert?" The pudgy-faced man knotted his fingers together on the table before him.

"We can fight, Padre." The man in the frock coat fidgeted and looked away from the piercing brown eyes. The Reverend Theodore Fitzhugh was the pastor of the small Presbyterian church in the nearby town. It made him uncomfortable to be addressed by a Catholic title, but he could never bring himself to tell the hawk-faced line manager of the South-Western Stage Company that. Some of the toughest mankillers ever to walk the West had managed stagecoach lines. James Odelbert was known to have killed three men, and more were whispered of. He was far from the weakest of his hard breed.

The red-haired attorney eyed Odelbert, head cocked to one side. "How do you propose we do that, sir?"

"Only one way I know to do that, James." He leaned forward, eyes blazing. "Get guns. Use 'em. Old man Silver's son, now—*he's* got the right idea."

Reverend Fitzhugh pursed his lips. "David Silver is a fugitive from justice," he said primly. "Surely you don't think it necessary to resort to *his* methods."

"I don't know if I'd call him a fugitive from *justice*, Theodore," Wilson James, the lanky attorney, remarked in a tone as dry as the dusty road that ran past Hugo's to the small town of Las Peñas, New Mexico Territory, two miles away. "That's a commodity that's been in rather short supply in our fair city of late."

Francis Warren, editor and publisher of the Las Peñas *Intelligencer*, laid down the ravaged skeleton of his chicken and mopped his pudgy features with a monogrammed handkerchief. "This talk of violence makes me quite queasy," he said. "Violence is no way to settle matters."

"Man commonly finds things real settled-like," drawled James Odelbert, "when he's dead."

Reverend Fitzhugh folded his pale hands before him. "Violence only breeds more violence," he said. " 'Vengeance is mine, saith the Lord.' We must exhaust every other possibility before resorting to the sword."

"But, Rev, *we're* exhausted," Odelbert exclaimed. "Men shot down in the streets, women raped in their homes, any man's property up for grabs if one of Durán's boys takes a fancy to it, a good man hunted like a dog for defending himself." He shook his head. "While we're sortin' through the rights and the wrongs and the proper way of doin' this and that, people are hurtin'."

"Ve're ready to defend ourselfs, gentlemen." The innkeeper emerged from the kitchen, wiping his hands on a towel. He was a stocky man, a Dutchman, several inches shorter than his Mexican wife, with a round face, sweeping black mustache, thinning, graying hair combed straight back on his cannonball head. "The people of Las Peñas, ve take too much already, I think."

"But we can't!" Warren burst out. "It would mean war—blood in the streets. It'd be Lincoln County all over again."

"Damn it, Warren, ain't it better to die fast on our feet than bleed to death on our knees?" Odelbert shouted. His face was flushed with angry blood.

"Surely there must be a better way," Fitzhugh said. He sipped his pop nervously through pursed lips.

James tilted his head and fixed the publisher with his gaze. "Have you any suggestions, Francis?"

Warren looked around. Hugo Ballenkamp had sat down beside Jim Odelbert on the long bench. The publisher read uncompromising determination on both faces, stark in the light of kerosene lanterns.

"I grant you the local authorities are of no help," he began. Ignoring Odelbert's derisive snort, he went on, gathering momentum. "But there is still a territorial government in Santa Fe. If we petition the governor, he'll send special investigators—troops perhaps. They'll set matters right."

"We must not take the law into our own hands," Fitzhugh said. "That would make us no better than Durán and his Forty Thieves."

The door of the common room flew open. A cold draft gusted through the room, pungent with piñon smoke from the kitchen chimney. Odelbert's hand went to the well-worn grip of the Wells Fargo model Smith & Wesson .45 at his hip. All heads snapped around, faces going white in sudden apprehension. A man stood there, thin-cheeked and sunken-eyed, in jeans and a denim jacket. The stage line manager took his hand from his pistol. "Ah, Manuel," Hugo said with a gusty sigh, recognizing his stablehand. "You should not scare us like dot."

Manuel said nothing. Instead he began to lean forward. The motion continued into a full-length fall, facedown on the sawdust-scattered planks of the floor.

The polished-bone handle of a bowie knife jutted from between his shoulder blades. The back of his jacket was a purple blotch of blood.

A looming shape filled the open door, stepped quickly inside. It was a huge man, almost seven feet tall, wearing a sheepskin jacket, with a red handkerchief knotted around a tree-trunk neck. He had a massively ugly face—coarse, big-nosed, and scarred grotesquely, as if chiseled from granite by a sculptor who was mad or drunk. He wore a Stetson pushed well back on his head. A Winchester was cradled like a child's toy in his hands. The hilt of a machete slung across his back jutted above the slope of his right shoulder. A bowie knife with a sixteen-inch blade was thrust through his belt. The haft digging into the overhang of his paunch was mate to the one jutting from the hired man's back.

Ballenkamp leapt to his feet. His blue eyes blazed with pallid fire. "Vot you do here, Abadón?" he demanded.

The big man ignored him. "I got a complaint," he said in a thick-tongued voice, heavy with mocking humor. "This *joto* here, he didn't want to take care of our horses. I really think you shoulda taught him better manners, señor."

Two more men stepped over the cooling corpse. One of them was a compact black man in chaps, leather vest, and a flat-brimmed black hat, holding a sawed-off double-barreled shotgun carelessly in one hand. The other was a lanky youth with a shock of white-blond hair that refused to be restrained by his hat. A blue scarf was knotted around his neck. His hands, black gloved, rested on twin cartridge belts slung around narrow hips, ominously close to the walnut grips of a pair of Remington New Model Army .44s, worn with the holsters tied down.

"M-murderers," gasped Reverend Fitzhugh. His lips were pressed to a thin white line.

"You've gone too far this time, Abadón," gritted Wilson James. "Not even Duran's store-bought police chief can overlook this—this cold-blooded butchery."

Abadón smiled, displayed a set of flawlessly white, even teeth. The contrast of their perfection to the battered brutality of his face was a physical shock. "Now, Señor James—"

A wild scream from the door to the kitchen cut him off. The three intruders gaped at Mrs. Ballenkamp, who stood with fists dug into the hollows beneath her prominent cheekbones, staring at Manuel's body.

It was the break Jim Odelbert had been waiting for. Quick as a serpent his hand was on the butt of the Smith & Wesson, the steel barrel sliding effortlessly from well-oiled leather. . . .

Two shots crashed out, echoing deafeningly from the low smoke-blackened beams of the taproom. Odelbert spun around, the pistol clattering to the floor. He clutched once, spasmodically, at Hugo Ballenkamp's upper arm. Then he slid lifelessly to the floor, leaving twin red trails of blood slimed down the front of the innkeeper's vest and trousers.

For a moment Ballenkamp stared in wide-eyed horror at the grinning pale-haired youth, who was holding a smoking Remington negligently between thumb and forefinger. Then the stout innkeeper turned and raced for the door, shouting, "María! Run!"

Abadón shot him in the back. He fell forward, but kept scrabbling ahead on hands and knees. Grimacing in irritation, he huge man brought the rifle to his shoulder and fired twice more. Blood gouted from the innkeep's mouth as the bullets slammed him into the floor. His wife shrieked and fled.

Attorney Wilson James had his right hand in the pocket of his coat, going for the short-barreled Colt he carried there. The black cowpuncher flipped up the shotgun and fired. The front of the lawyer's beige silk waistcoat exploded in a red shower. James flew backwards. His head slammed against the slate mantelpiece. He collapsed. One hand slumped loosely into the fireplace. A fresh stink joined the odor of burned powder and spilled blood as the hungry flames crisped the short red hairs on the back of his hand.

Moving with grace and speed that belied his bulk, Abadón ran across the common room, vaulted over Ballenkamp's body, and raced into the kitchen in pursuit of the innkeep's wife, drawing his machete as he ran. Francis Warren screamed as the black pivoted on his heel and blew the Reverend Theodore Fitzhugh's head into a mist of blood and clotted brains that spattered the publisher's shoulder and face. Warren dived under the table.

"I'm dry," the black cowboy drawled. "Looks like you got to drag ol' Fat Frank out by the heels, Slowhand."

The towheaded youth grinned a slow wide grin. "Nah," he said. He raised his Remington and fired once without seeming to aim.

A splinter flew from the thick tabletop as the .44 punched through it. A heartbeat later there was a thump. The black man looked into the slightly protuberant water-blue eyes of Francis Warren. They didn't meet his gaze. The dime-sized hole between them meant they never would. "Not bad," the shotgunner said. "Not too fucking bad."

They heard the clump of Marcosio Abadón's boots in the kitchen and looked up to see him enter, machete in hand. The broad, blunt blade dripped red. Several strands of long black hair were stuck to it, glued in the blood. "You finish those fuckers?"

"Yeah," Slowhand McVie replied. The black just nodded.

Abadón walked to the outer door, waving one heavy hand at the gray-blue gunsmoke that hung in the air in acrid bands. "All right, Claude," he called out into the night. "We're done in here. Start bringin' the dynamite."

The trim black had his shotgun broken open and was placing brown-paper cartridges fastidiously in the breech of his double-gun. "What about the kike?" he asked.

Abadón gestured around him at the bloodied corpses littering the tavern. "I don' think he's gonna give us any more trouble. What do *you* think, *cuate*?" And throwing his huge head back he began to laugh.

CHAPTER TWO

"Oh, honey," the tiny woman chirped. "Oh honey, that feels so fine!"

Raider turned his head on the pillow. Tangled brown hair covered his face, tickling his nose. He slid his hands down from Mrs. Hannah Parker's sharp shoulder blades to her small hard ass and buried himself full length inside her.

She gasped. Her hands clawed at his back. He stiffened as her nails dug into the powerful V-shaped muscles. Then she sucked in a frantic breath and snapped her pussy noose-tight around his probing manhood. He felt his eyes bug out and began to ramrod her for all he was worth.

The woman moaned and commenced gnawing at his neck. Her rump started to rotate in his hands. He felt her nipples hard and hot against his chest. He tried to kiss her, got a mouthful of hair, tried again and got her on the forehead. Her skin tasted of salty sweat.

It was a seedy St. Louis hotel room, with peeling pin-striped wallpaper stained in huge patches like sweat beneath the arms of a dockwalloper's shirt. It sported a single chair and a crook-legged stand holding a battered tin bowl under a cracked fly-specked shard of a mirror, a window that looked out on an alley and the back of a derelict warehouse, and the one rump-sprung bed on which the naked pair wrestled and groaned their passion. The man's clothes were flung in a heap by the bed. A faded brown dress, frequently patched and meticulously clean, was folded neatly on the chair, with an orderly pile of frilly ladies' underthings atop it.

She was a widow who worked as a seamstress out of a tiny cubicle above an attorney's office not far from the Mississippi waterfront. As luck would have it, the attorney was cooperating with the Pinkerton National Detective Agency in trying to bust up a ring of latter-day river pirates operating on the Mississippi. Assigned to the case with his chubby, dapper, blond-haired partner, Doc Weatherbee, Raider had struck up an acquaintance with the diminutive birdlike woman he met coming out of lawyer Clete Magnusson's building one June afternoon.

A rangy six-footer with the build, straight jet-black hair, and aquiline features of a Plains warrior, a rakish mustache, and the devil in his dark brown eyes, Raider was a natural to take the eye of any healthy young woman, and a good many who weren't so young.

Why little Mrs. Parker had caught Raider's attention was another question. He was partial to big, creamy-skinned, buxom blondes of questionable virtue—in fact, he didn't mind if there wasn't a question in the world as to their virtue, nor did dark roots in a fine head of gold hair put him off his stride, especially if that head was bobbing up and down over his rigid cock.

But Hannah Parker was practically the opposite of what his tastes ran to. She was tiny, even for a woman, and even late nineteenth-century frontier gallantry would find it hard to call her anything but skinny. Her breasts weren't large. She was sharp-featured, mousy-haired, with a naturally brown complexion. But she was pretty in a miniature kind of way, with a lively cricket manner, incredibly bright hazel eyes, and a smile that filled her face with a vibrant elfin beauty. And she was very, very lonely.

Also, she screwed like a crazed mink.

She was losing all control now, her strong slender thighs clamping Raider's narrow waist like bands of iron, her fingernails digging furrows in his sides, moaning and nip-

ping him on the neck. ''Rade! Oh, Raider, you're so big!
You'll tear me apart!''

He was taking her in a sweaty, pulse-pounding haze.
The smell and feel and taste of her were driving him crazy.
He felt as if he were just going to bust at any minute. He
could only hunch himself into her with all the strength of
his back and belly muscles and wonder how it could keep
feeling better and better as he was swept up and rushed
inexorably onward to an explosion of delight . . .

Knock, knock at the door. ''Telegram for Mr. Raider,''
in a nasal adolescent voice.

''Oh, baby, don't stop, don't slow down, I'm close,
sooo close.''

''Go the hell away!''

Knock, knock. ''Telegram.''

''Yes, ah! Keep it up! Oh, more, more, oh yes, oh
yes!''

''Go *away*! I'm—oh, *gawd*—busy!''

Knockknockknock. ''It says it's urgent, Mr. Raider. It's
from a Mr. Wagner in Chicago.''

''Ah! Ah! Oh, honey! Aaaah!''

''They told me at the desk that you had to have this
right now, Mr. Raider.''

Hannah's strong belly was churning, her cunt milking
Raider's prick like urgent fingers. His eyes filled with
stinging sweat. As the insistent bellhop rapped his knuckles against the door again, Raider wormed his hand out
from under the woman's satiny, sweat-shiny butt, reached
over to the warped and peeling chair sitting beside the bed,
and drew his Peacemaker from the holster slung over its
hoop-shaped back.

''Mr. *Raider*,'' the bellhop whined.

Raider raised the heavy Colt and fired once into the top
of the doorjamb. There was a high-pitched wail of terror,
followed by the patter of running feet, dwindling along the
hallway.

Hannah's eyes were open wide. ''Rade—what?'' But

her hips never quit pumping, and her quim never slackened its grip on him.

He slipped the pistol back in the holster. "Nothin'," he grunted. He wedged his hand between their naked bodies and grabbed a tit. It was small and cone-shaped. He squeezed the nipple between thumb and forefinger and pulled her against him with the hand cupped around her muscular butt cheek. Her eyes rolled up and an animal cry escaped from her throat as she came.

Crushing her against him, he wagged his lean rump from side to side as his prick spurted into her in great, heart-stopping jolts. It was like having the breath crushed from him by a giant hand. His whole body tensed under the onslaught of wave after wave of relentless pleasure.

Finally the wild passion of mutual orgasm eased its grip. He lay atop her, wholly spent. She stroked his tousled black hair. "Oh, Raider, honey," she said huskily, her eyes glowing up at his. "I've never known anyone like you."

"Never knowed anybody like you," he muttered—bashfully, because it was true. She hugged him and kissed his black-stubbled cheek.

The door burst in.

Raider reared his upper body like a sidewinder rising off a flat rock. A slope-shouldered hulk stood there in a gray serge sack coat, with shapeless black trousers, a flowered vest, and a Russian model Smith & Wesson slung low on his right hip, glowering with pig eyes over a mashed pug's nose and a walrus mustache. Foggily Raider recognized the bouncer from the saloon downstairs. At the big man's elbow stood a blue-clad wisp of a bellhop, bouncing in agitation from one foot to another and chattering, "He *shot* at me, he actually tried to *shoot* me!" in an indignant squeak.

"Now, just what in hell did you mean—" the hulk began. Then his small eyes lit on the nude figure of Mrs. Parker, reclining among the disordered sheets. She gazed at him in a daze of repleted lust, too spent even for the normal reflex of modesty to take control. He turned the color of boiled beets.

"Um, er, beg yer pardon, ma'am," he stammered, and backed out the door. The jittering bellhop started to protest. The bouncer put a hand the size of a carpetbag over the bellhop's pinched face and shoved him back out of the doorway.

The door shut with feathery lightness.

"Jesus Christ!" Raider muttered. He jumped off the bed and started pulling on his drawers.

"What's happening, Raider honey?" Hannah asked muzzily.

"That big yahoo's out there tryin' to collect what few wits God give him," he said. "When he does, he's gonna be back with blood in his eye."

She sat up, pulling a corner of the sheet up before her. "Can't you reason with him?" One small breast, dark-nippled, peeked out coyly from behind the sheet.

"Never try to reason with nobody whose head comes to a ol' point on top," Raider replied. He looked at her appreciatively for a moment, then let his gaze wander to take in the heavy brass bedstead. "Git on up off'n there, honey. I need to move the bed over here in front of this here door."

"I'm warnin' you now, Mr. Raider," the house detective called through the door. "Give yourself up peaceable-like or we'll have to come in there and drag you out."

"Blow it out yer—er, forgit it, mister," came Raider's voice back, muffled by the wood of the door.

The dick was a small, trim man, with lank black hair slicked across his round skull and held down by a derby, and ears that stood out like jug handles. He frowned and chewed his mustache. "Gonna have to bust down the door," he observed.

"But he's got a gal in there!" exclaimed the bouncer.

"But he's got a gun!" exclaimed the bellhop.

The detective twisted his gold watch fob thoughtfully in

his fingers. "Only other choice is to call the police. And you know they're always lookin' for excuses to shut us down."

The bellhop, who had a good thing going attending to the needs of sweet-toothed guests who wanted some nice tarts with their whiskey, looked at the bouncer. The bouncer, who dealt monte in the back room and sometimes slipped a little something extra in the drink of a customer who seemed to be toting round more ready cash than was good for him, returned the look.

"Bust the door down," the bouncer said.

The detective took off his coat and hung it from the doorknob of the room across from Raider's. Beneath it he was wearing a plain gray silk vest and a Colt in a shoulder rig. "Give a hand here, Joe," he said to the broken-nosed bouncer. The pug tossed away his own coat. Muscles rippled visibly beneath his none-too-clean shirt as he and the detective put their shoulders to the door. The bellhop, a skinny youth with prematurely thinning blond hair and no perceptible chin, stood by wringing his hands.

"Good afternoon, gentlemen," a pleasant voice said from down the corridor. "What seems to be the problem?"

They turned their heads to see a man standing a few feet away. He wasn't tall, nor short, but middle-sized, with blond hair and innocent blue eyes looking from a boyish, plump face. He wore a black derby set at a jaunty angle, blue coat and trousers of obviously fine cut and quality, and a black vest. His linen was spotless and crisp. He carried an ebony cane with an inlaid silver knob for a head. He looked soft. Harmless.

The big pug growled. "Having a little difficulty with one of our guests," murmured the hotel dick. He wasn't paid good money to talk sideways to sharp-dressed slickers. "He took a shot at Jerry here whilst he was tryin' to deliver a telegram."

"As if it's any of your business," the bellhop said tartly.

The newcomer gave him a mild look. "I don't see any bullet holes in the door," he observed.

The bouncer had straightened up from the door and was scowling down at the smaller man. The embarrassment of his earlier retreat from Raider's room was starting to sting. "Want I should pitch him down the stairs, Hank?"

The dick waved a negative hand. "Reckon he fired into the jamb."

"I see." The blond man nodded. He held the cane up before his chest and wagged a finger encased in a pigskin glove. "So he doesn't appear to have been making a serious assault on your compatriot. Nor has he done severe damage. Perhaps, if I were permitted to try to reason with him, we could defuse the situation without any, ah, untoward incident."

The dick started to ask why in hell's name the dude thought he could talk sense into the crazy man in Room 323. Before he could, the bellhop, who had been looking forward to seeing the ex-pug Joe pound some respect into the man—imagine, he'd actually *shot* at him!—piped up, "You keep out of this! Make him butt out, Joe."

"I wonder," the blond man said, "why the man in this room fired the shot to begin with? Perhaps the bellhop did something to aggravate him?"

Jerry turned red. "Shut him up, Joe!"

Meanwhile the wheels in the bouncer's brain had been turning with their customary ponderousness. He very much wanted to hit somebody, that being the best cure he knew for embarrassment. Now, the man in 323 was toting some heavy iron, and not even the man they used to call Fightin' Joe Turner thought he could hit harder than a .44-40 slug. This soft eastern-looking dude, on the other hand . . .

Moving with surprising speed for a man of his bulk, Fightin' Joe stepped forward. His hamhock-sized right hand pistoned toward the chubby line of the blond man's jaw.

The interloper ducked under the blow. The breath exploded in a foul-smelling gust from Fightin' Joe's lungs as the dapper man rammed the tip of his cane into the ex-boxer's solar plexus. Joe doubled. The blond man stepped alongside him and rapped him smartly on the back of the skull with the knob of his cane. Big Joe went down in a heap.

"Now," the blond man said, straightening, "if you'll permit me . . ." The detective, standing by with his thumbs hooked into the armholes of his vest, nodded. His tongue scoured slowly around the inside of his cheek. The bellhop cowered away as the newcomer stepped up to the door marked 323 in faded gold ink and rapped with the head of the cane.

"Go 'way," growled a voice. It was a voice that had seen considerable punishment at the hands of whiskey in the interval since the bellhop and the bouncer had walked in on its owner and his friend. Having gotten himself into this fix stone cold sober, Raider had seen no reason to face the consequences in that condition.

"It's Doc," the blond man said.

"Don'—don't know nobody by that name."

"It's agency business," Doc Weatherbee said sharply. "It's urgent."

A moment while Raider's strong sense of duty worked against the whiskey. Then, "I'm coming." The men in the hallway heard the scrape of the bedstead being moved away from the door.

Doc looked to the detective. "This man's my partner. I assure you he'll cause no further disturbance. If you must insist on pressing charges, I'll be glad to go bail for him."

The small man's mouth curved beneath his mustache in a slow, sour smile. "Reckon the hotel can survive a bullet hole in the door jamb," he drawled. He turned to the prostrate form of Fightin' Joe, who was stirring and groaning, and booted him in the ribs. "C'mon, git a move on. You too, Jerry—ain't you got some pimpin' to do?"

"You stupid son of a bitch," Doc hissed as he steered Raider through the faded magnificence of the lobby of the

Hotel Royale. It had taken every bit of Doc's considerable store of charm to get Hannah Parker calmed down and safely on her way, and he was starting to feel frayed around the edges. "Why'd you have to go and start a ruckus?"

Raider winced. "Don't go ridin' me, Doc," he whined. "That little nancy-boy of a bellhop done walked in on me while I was puttin' it to h-hic-Hannah. Couldn't let him git away with *that*, could I?"

The rangy man blubbered a little. Doc wondered how much whiskey he'd sucked up in the short time he'd had. Usually it took hours of hard drinking to get his partner maudlin and teary.

The stage after that was red-eyed fighting drunk. *Better keep him away from the sauce*, the dapper Pinkerton told himself.

Raider fetched up against a pillar, stopped, and patted it as if to reassure himself of its solidity. It was oak, carved with grooves running up it and flowering at the top into big cone-shaped leaves, an imitation of the columns found in the ancient Egyptian temples that had been under excavation since early in the century, which were carved to resemble bundles of papyrus reeds. The Royale had been built in the thirties, during the big boom of Mississippi traffic, as well as an early vogue for Egyptology. In its day it had possessed a certain gaudy splendor. The gilt had long since begun to flake off the capitals of the mock-Egyptian columns that grew like a well-ordered orchard in the big lobby, but the hotel still hung to what pretentions of grandeur it could—as witness the fact that it still had a complement, small and surly as it was, of bellhops.

"Wh-whass the all-fired hurry, anyway?" Raider demanded as he navigated cautiously around the enameled pillar.

"We've got a job. There's going to be another operative in on it with us. She's waiting for us in the restaurant."

Raider dug his heels into threadbare carpet printed with

faded pyramids and sphinxes. "She? *She*? Old Allan expects us to work with a *woman*?"

Heads turned as the drummers and bummers loitering on the cracked leather-covered chairs of the lobby craned their necks to see what was going on. Doc shushed his partner frantically. "For God's sake, Rade, the agency's always used female operatives."

"I ain't never held with that, neither," proclaimed Raider, wagging his head from side to side like an angry bull. "A petticoat doin' a man's work—what does Chicago think we are, anyway? Wet nurses?"

"Jesus, Raider—" But the tall man had jerked away and gone striding toward the gilded papyrus-bundle arch that led into the restaurant.

Wincing, Doc followed, trotting like an apprehensive terrier.

When he caught up with his partner, Raider was standing spraddle-legged in the foyer, ignoring the balding waiter in shiny black pants and sleeve garters who was hovering nearby asking him if he wished to take a seat. The restaurant hadn't started to fill up with its lunchtime customers yet, not that it ever got much to speak of. A few salesmen with shiny seats to their trousers sat around peering at their papers through bloodshot eyes, and a pair of Germans who'd wandered in to escape the late-morning heat sat in a corner arguing loudly and unintelligibly over foaming steins of lager beer.

A woman dressed in a brown suit and a white blouse with a flounce in the front sat by herself across the dingy dining room, studying a folded newspaper and drinking tea. A jaunty little hat sporting a single pheasant feather was perched atop high-piled auburn hair. The suit was exquisitely tailored, and did full justice to the exquisite figure beneath.

Raider strode uncertainly across to her, the fringes of his buckskin jacket flapping. She looked up from her copy of the *Weekly Democrat* as he approached. Her eyes were green. The look in them was distinctly cool.

"Wha—whaddya mean?" Raider blurted, collapsing into a chair across from her. "A gal like you, in a place like this without an escort. It ain't—urp—ain't *fitten*."

She arched a slim tapered brow. "Operative Raider, I presume?"

Doc winced again as he pulled out the chair beside Raider and plumped his broad bottom down. The woman's tone of voice had icicles dripping from it, like a roof gutter in January.

"We're both having coffee," he said pointedly to the waiter, who had trotted to the table in Raider's wake. He turned to his partner. "Rade," he said, trying to sound cheerfully businesslike. "I'd like you to meet Operative Judy Holiday. Miss Holiday, this is Operative Raider."

"I've heard *so* much about you," she said, eyeing the inebriated agent as she would a snake she'd spotted lying across her path: as if trying to make up her mind whether to beat it to death with her walking stick or just detour around and be on her way. "The stories did you full justice, it seems."

Raider sunk his head down inside the collar of his shirt and stared at her blearily, obviously unable to make heads or tails of what she said. Abruptly his brow creased in a scowl.

"That worthless little pimp—oh, pardon my language, Miss Holiday, I fergot myself. That lousy little bastard of a bellhop had a telegram for me when he come waltzin' in whilst I was—that is, he had a telegram fer me, and he ain't never given it to me."

July Holiday was elaborately ignoring him. "Never mind that," Doc said desperately. He mopped his forehead with a monogrammed handkerchief, blotting up a shiny mosaic of sweat that wasn't caused by the sticky Missouri heat alone. He stuffed the kerchief back in his vest pocket and pulled out a crumpled yellow form and tossed it on the spotted linen tablecloth. "I got the same one. It's from Wagner. We're going to New Mexico Territory. Miss Holiday's got the details."

The waiter arrived with two cups of coffee. Doc gulped his and waited for Raider to resume his denunciation of the practice of employing female agents. But his partner appeared to have forgotten his earlier objections. Instead he was staring with moist calf's eyes at the impressive swelling of Judy Holiday's bodice. He reminded Doc of an infant with lunch on its mind.

Holiday's full lips closed into a firm line. "If you're *quite sure* your partner is in a condition hear the terms of our commission," she said. "I'd certainly hate to put him to the inconvenience of overtaxing his mental faculties."

Raider waved a hand indulgently. "Don't trouble your pretty li'l head about any of that," he said with a sappy smile. "Just spit them details right on out, and don't hold back none on my account."

The telegram from Chicago lying on the table in front of him had long since had the crispness sweated out of it. Doc was beginning to know what it felt like. His partner was never what an honest man would call a model of elegance. On the other hand, he had a Westerner's rough gallantry, and a good sight more than that with any woman he wanted to charm. Aside from her unfeminine-seeming choice of profession, the beautiful Miss Holiday was a good example of the type Raider would be dead set on charming—right out of her clothes, if he could.

Doc wouldn't have minded getting Judy Holiday into a state of nature either. But he'd no sooner had the thought, when he'd seen the female agent coming down the gangplank of the river steamer that morning, than he'd dismissed the possibility from his mind. She was courteous in a brisk, professional way, but she had a way of talking with a man without giving him any encouragement. She wasn't the sort to toss her tail up over her cruppers for the first stud to come around arching his neck and prancing, even one as sound of wind and limb as Raider. With him practically slobbering all over himself, it was clearly all Judy Holiday could do to sit at the same table with him.

The woman set her shoulders and laid the newspaper

down before her. "I was just reading an account that pertains to our case, gentlemen." There was just the slightest catch before "gentlemen." "It will give you a notion of our brief. If you'd be so good as to read it to our associate, Dr. Weatherbee?"

Doc picked up the paper, drew a pair of round reading glasses from an inside pocket of his coat, propped them on the end of his nose, and squinted at the uppermost page. "'A Tragedy in New Mexico Territory,' " he read from the article neatly outlined in pencil. Pausing, he glanced over the top of his spectacles at Holiday. "It must be quite a tragedy, if the *Democrat*'s taking notice of goings-on in New Mexico."

"Keep reading."

"'Fiery Explosion of Town-House Claims Seven Lives,' " Doc read. "'The serenity of the sleepy mountain village of Las Peñas, New Mexico Territory, was shattered in a hideous fashion in the nocturnal hours of April 15, by an explosion which destroyed Ballenkamp's Roadhouse, which lies on the highway leading west to Las Vegas. Struck down by the tragedy were Wilson James, a lawyer; Francis Warren, publisher; the Reverend Theodore Fitzhugh of the First Presbyterian Church of Las Peñas; James Odelbert, regional manager for the South-Western Stage Company; Hugo Ballenkamp, the publican, a German; his wife María, a Mexican; and Manuel Rivas, Mr. Ballenkamp's stableman.

"'William Broward, police chief of Las Peñas, placed the blame for the calamity on dynamite which Ballenkamp kept stored in a shed behind his tavern, to use in keeping his property clear of stumps. Chief Broward was at a loss to say why the German had in his possession dynamite sufficient to cause a blast of such magnitude.

"'A special memorial service was held in the First Presbyterian Church Sunday last in memory of the Reverend Fitzhugh and his fellow unfortunate victims.' "

He laid the paper down, folded the specs, and tucked them away in his coat. "A grim account."

Awash though his brain was in booze, Raider had not wholly forgotten his trade. "Where do we come in?" he slurred.

"The South-Western Stage Company has engaged the services of the agency," Miss Holiday said, folding her hands before her. "It seems they're less than satisfied that the explosion was accidental."

"That's a hell—er, a heck of a lot of dynamite to have around for blowin' out stumps and such," Raider observed.

"It seems that Mr. Odelbert reported that a gang of criminals was running the town, and that the authorities were helpless to do anything about it," Holiday said. "Odelbert was apparently unable to guarantee the safety of passengers and parcels carried by his line. He told his superiors that if things continued he'd be forced to take matters into his own hands; he seems to have been an impetuous sort."

Doc set his jaw and drew up his upper lip, exposing his even white teeth. "Seven people dead? Just to rub out one man? That's pretty foul, even for foul play."

"That's why the South-Western Stage Company is willing to pay for an investigation."

Raider shifted in his chair. He was still slouched like a sack of potatoes, but his gaze was sharper and clearer than it had been when he'd first sat down. "Whyn't they appeal to the terr'torial government?"

Holiday arched a brow skeptically. "This is New Mexico we're speaking of, Mr. Raider."

"Lew Wallace is too busy writing books to be corrupt," Doc, fairminded as always, pointed out. "And his successor hasn't even arrived in Santa Fe yet. But you know as well as I do what a long gray beard a man can grow waiting for justice from the Santa Fe ring that runs the territory." In the wake of the Lincoln County War, old warhorse Lew Wallace, who had served the Union with some distinction during the Civil War, had been appointed governor of New Mexico Territory to clean the place up. He'd been president of the court of inquiry that condemned

Wirz, commandant of Andersonville, and had helped try the alleged conspirators in the Lincoln assassination, and could scarcely be accused of being overly lenient. What he'd done had been to write *Ben Hur*, while the territory went on pretty much as always. On the other hand, *Ben Hur* was a big best-seller, and what was then called the New Mexico Territory had a tradition of civic corruption stretching unbroken over three centuries, so maybe he had the right idea.

Raider frowned profoundly. "Sendin' a woman into a nest of vipers like that . . ." he grumbled, and shook his head. " 'Tain't hardly right."

Holiday bristled. "I have served the Pinkerton National Detective Agency for some three years now, and with some distinction, if I may lay false modesty aside. I have impersonated a nurse, a factory worker, an heiress, and a whore, among other roles I have assumed in service of the agency. I have helped apprehend embezzlers, arsonists, bank robbers, and murderers. I have been personally commended by Mr. Allan Pinkerton on three occasions. So forgive me for being so bold, Raider, but I feel I am quite as competent to tend to the agency's interests—and fend for myself—as any, any—any dissolute booze-fighter in a buckskin jacket!"

She stood up with an angry rustle of crinolines. "Doctor, you know where to find me. I am ready to depart for the territory this very day—if you can get your partner sober enough to travel!"

She flounced out of the restaurant. Heads had turned at her outburst. They swiveled to follow her as she stormed out, curiosity giving way to raw admiration. "You made a hell of a first impression, Rade," Doc said bitterly, slumping in his chair. "It's going to be a real pleasure, this assignment. I can tell already."

Raider was staring after the departed operative with his mouth hanging open beneath his drooping mustache. "I'll . . . be . . . damned," he said with the slow precision of the drunk who wishes to make sure he's understood.

"No question of that," Doc agreed.

Raider sat back and nodded abruptly, jutting his chin out, like a military hero cast in bronze on horseback. "She loves me," he announced. "I could see it in her eyes."

"Oh, Jesus Christ on a bicycle." Doc put his head in his hands for a moment, rubbing his eyes with the heels. When he lifted his head again the light of determination shone in his pale blue eyes. "Waiter," he called. "A bottle of your best whiskey, such as it may be."

Raider looked at him in slightly cross-eyed surprise. "Thought you was in a hurry to get started, like that fine li'l chestnut filly."

Doc shook his head. "I have some important preparation for the mission to do."

"How you gonna do that, with a bottle of rotgut?"

"I'm going to get stinking drunk."

CHAPTER THREE

Creaking and jingling and groaning, swaying from side to side like a China clipper under all plain sail, a wagon trundled down the rough dirt track from the mountains. It passed the tall ponderosa pine that stood by itself on the rise above the Taylor place, and started down the long slope to Las Peñas with a squeal of the brake, past the strangely shaped and massive granite outcrops that dotted the slopes and meadows hereabouts and gave the town its name. A single mule, with a long-suffering expression and a straw hat perched on her head to shield her eyes from the bright mountain sunlight, plodded in the harness. A sprig of early spring flowers was stuck in the band of the hat, and the mule's long ears stuck through holes cut in the brim. The ears wagged as the animal's head bobbed up and down to the slow rhythm of her walk.

A man sat in the box of the wagon, holding the reins and a buggy whip negligently in one hand. He was a plump-looking fellow, the fullness of his figure perhaps enhanced by the black and white checked traveling suit he wore. He had a derby perched to the side of his blond head, and a cheroot in his mouth. He was singing to himself.

Manny Rodríguez, aged ten, and his sister Isabel, eight, were walking down the hill to pay a visit to some friends in town when the wagon came by. They stopped to watch the outlandish sight with open mouths. It was a compact

Studebaker with a gleaming white canvas canopy, hung around with an assortment of kegs and crates and sacks. The letters AOA were painted prominently on the side of the wagon, and arcing over them the legend: ACME OVERLAND APOTHECARY, in the frilly sort of block letters circus handbills used. Colored pennants streamed from the canopy and the wagon's body.

"Good morning, *muchacho y muchacha*," the blond man called with a cheery wave.

Manny and his sister waved back. The wagon passed with a clatter and a jingle. A placard in the back of the wagon proclaimed: "Doctor Weatherbee's Patented Egyptian Cure: The Secret of the Pharaohs," and displayed a camel and a pair of palm trees, with the pyramids in the background. Egypt was a big number in 1881, too. Manny read the placard, forming the words with his lips. He read English, having learned how in school, but these words meant nothing to him. There was a mysterious taste to them, though. Tantalizing.

He grabbed his sister's hand and began to run after the wagon.

By the time the wagon rumbled into the central plaza and halted beneath a cottonwood whose limbs were fuzzed with green leaf buds, a whole mob of children, laughing and shouting, had joined the motley cavalcade. A sizable number of adults had collected too, though they were careful to walk deliberately and keep clear of the mass of children. Las Peñas was nowhere in particular; it didn't see a sight like the gaudy AOA wagon every day of the year.

The blond man laid down the reins and stood up. The mule sighed and wrinkled her nose in distaste at her surroundings. The village was a collection of blocky adobe houses for the most part, though the more pretentious structures, which tended to cluster in the southern half of town, were frame. The buildings around the plaza were wood, or at least equipped with wooden false fronts. The town even sported a modest Town Hall, across the tree-lined plaza from where the wonderful wagon was parked, with a white portico and fluted white pilasters to either side—all carved of wood, of course. Las Peñas was far from grand enough to have a marble facade on its town hall, or even one of good cut granite.

The blond man cleared his throat. "Children of Las Peñas, a very good morning to you! Dr. Weatherbee, Miracle Healer and Master of Egyptian Mysteries, has come among you!" The children laughed and clapped. What he was saying meant little to them, but they loved the pompous yet at the same time cheerful way he had of saying it. "Let your mothers and fathers, your uncles and your aunts, know that I have come, to heal the sick and strengthen the infirm, with my Patented Egyptian Cure, available at the nominal sum of one dollar a bottle, and a myriad other healing wonders. My assistant and I will reveal the Secrets of the Orient, in an instructive and entertaining Lecture to be presented this evening at seven o'clock. Come one, come all, to hear the Wisdom of the Ancients, as well as the latest information on modern hygiene. See the lovely Madame Teresa perform the mysterious Serpent Dance, charming a dangerous Reptile with Arcane Gestures. And more, ever so much more!"

The canopy flap stirred, and a woman came out onto the box. A sigh rose from the onlookers, mostly from males of the adult stage or thereabouts. She was dressed in a white peasant blouse and a full skirt, deep blue worked with embroidery of gold and red and white, with a scarlet sash about her narrow waist. Her green eyes were rimmed with kohl, making them huge, and her hair, glinting almost the color of copper in the sunlight, was confined in a gay scarf. She didn't look Egyptian, nor did she look Gypsy, though that was the effect intended in general—not that the citizens of Las Peñas knew what either breed of cat looked like. Mostly she was meant to look exotic, and that she did—especially the way the white blouse jutted out in front. She dipped hands that glittered with rings into pockets on the front of her dress, and scattered candies wrapped in twists of colored papers to the children, who scrambled for them shrieking with delight.

"Well now," the stocky big-bellied man with the bloodshot eyes who stood on the boardwalk beneath the awning of the Silver King Saloon said around the frayed stub of his cigar, "will you git a load of that, brother? A damn quack done brung his medicine show to our fair city. Some sheep gonna get sheared tonight!" He tipped back his heavy head and laughed. His mouth was wide and mobile.

He took the fat cigar stub from his mouth and eyed it. "But that little lady he's got with him—maybe I'll mosey on down for his show this evenin'." He scratched a lucifer alight on an upright and puffed his cigar into noisome life. "She's real somethin', ain't she?" he said through a cloud of blue smoke.

The tall dark-haired man who stood at his elbow shifted a few inches away from the billow of pungent smoke, turning his head slightly so the other wouldn't catch the look of disgust that flickered across his hawk's face. "Yep," he said.

"Wouldn't mind givin' that little Gypsy gal a try," the first man said, chewing on his cigar. "Give her a taste of ol' Clarence Redeye King, she's gonna want to run off *from* the circus."

He laughed uproariously at his own wit and pounded his comrade on the back with a broad black-nailed hand. The other grinned and nodded agreeably. But the grin didn't reach his Cheyenne-dark eyes. They held the image of the green-eyed, auburn-haired woman deep within them.

"C'mon, Raider, old buddy," the man called Redeye said, thumping the taller man on the shoulder blade. "I'll buy you a drink."

Raider's eyes relinquished Judy Holiday as reluctantly as a lover breaking an embrace. He followed the shorter, wider man into the cool darkness of the Silver King.

Back in the years following the Civil War a German prospector struck a promising vein of silver in the mountains north of town. The discovery brought a brief boom to isolated Las Peñas, nestled in the Mosca Picanda range that lay like a boundary wall between the Las Vegas Plateau, lying in the shadow of the lofty Sangre de Cristos, and the Raton Plateau in the east. Unfortunately the strike amounted to a solitary ledge, soon mined out, and held not a fleck more of anything more valuable than feldspar and quartz. The name of Las Peñas's foremost watering hole was a legacy of the short-lived optimism of those days.

Redeye steered his companion to a round table in a corner of the saloon and called for a bottle of whiskey. The bardog came out bearing a bottle of good Kentucky bourbon on a tray with two glasses. Raider raised an appreciative eyebrow as the barkeep, a glum shapeless character with a face that seemed to have been cobbled together from a bunch of potatoes, held up the brimful bottle for Redeye's inspection, like a white-tie waiter at Delmonico's presenting a fine vintage for the approval of some glittering swell. Redeye grinned an appreciative bloodhound smile.

"Thass okay, Henry. I trust you. You wouldn't try to palm off no bar-rag squeezin's on none of the boys." His gravel-toned voice was full of false camaraderie that failed to obscure the heavy undertone of threat. The bartender's lumpy face contorted briefly and he slouched off.

"That's the real stuff," said Raider, leaning forward and allowing just a touch of admiration to creep into his voice. "Reckon you pull some heavy weight around here, hombre."

Redeye laughed expansively. He twisted the cap off the bottle with his blunt fingers. "Well, there is some as says I'm a man o' parts—'specially the wimmenfolk, if you catch my drift, hey? hey?" He reached over and nudged Raider with his elbow, wrinkling his seamed bulldog face in a series of winks. "But it ain't just me alone, boy. This here's the new West. One man cain't pull near so much weight as a good solid bunch all haulin' together, if you get me."

"I allus done pretty good on my own," Raider said. He

watched Redeye slosh whiskey into a shot glass for him and tossed it back.

"Slow down, boy, that's the real stuff, just like you said. Not your common barroom bellywash." He raised his own glass and sipped.

"I don't doubt you allus done good ridin' a lone trail, Raider." The man was eyeing the tall Pink sidelong now, cunning glinting in his eyes. "You're a real steady feller, pegged you for one from the first. But times is changin', boy. Shorely you can see that."

"Reckon you lost me at the last bend," Raider murmured, letting the other pour him a fresh shot.

For all the studied disinterest of his exterior, Raider was drawn taut as piano wire inside. This was the moment he'd been waiting for—the nibble he'd been angling for since riding into Las Peñas almost a week before.

He was running his usual dodge, playing the role of a quiet drifter who everybody just sort of naturally took for a man who was looking to hire out the heavy Remington with the well-worn grip he wore low on his left hip in a cut-down cavalry holster. He took a room at Wideman's Hotel two blocks from the plaza and then sort of took in the scenery, making the rounds of the town's several bars, buying a few drinks, sitting in on card games that weren't too obviously rigged, showing enough coin that the town police wouldn't roust him for a vag. A typical gunslinger on the bum, looking for the angle, whether it was shoving muscle for some fat town boss or transferring livestock ownership by means of a lasso and a red-hot running iron. A hard man, and one not given to getting likkered up or shooting off his mouth. Like the man said, steady.

While he was settling into the sleepy round of life in Las Peñas, Raider kept his senses, naturally keen and well-honed by his Pinkerton training and years of experience, sharpened to pick up the situation in the little New Mexico town. What he found disturbed him. For Las Peñas was nowhere near the calm little burg where nothing had ever happened or ever would that it appeared on the surface.

It was a town that slept, waked, and worked under a pall of fear so thick and heavy you could almost see it, almost taste it, like the smoke plume downwind of a Pittsburgh foundry. Nothing very obvious. Just the drawn, pinched look on people's faces, as if it was quite some time since last they'd known untroubled sleep. Like the way all the women went around with their heads down, as if to hide their faces under the overhang of their sunbonnets, and always seemed in a hurry when they went out on the streets. Like the way that nobody went heeled in the town, except for the police with their silver stars—and the men who swaggered through the streets like soldiers of a conquering army, in groups of two or three or more, rarely alone, with their thumbs stuck in gunbelts stuffed with shiny cartridges and their heads held high. They all seemed to know each other, to greet one another on sight like members of some secret brotherhood.

The man who referred amiably to himself as Redeye was one of that select fraternity.

Just as he was giving the town the once-over, Raider was inspected in return. Again, it was nothing too obvious. The first day or so he was in town, the police kept a pretty close eye on him, though they never tried to talk him out of wearing his Peacemaker. Then their attention slacked off. At the same time, the secretive brotherhood had begun keeping an eye on him. Whenever he sat down in a bar, there was either one of the gun-toters there, or one or two showed up before his feet had got used to having the weight off. And there was always one of them in sight of his hotel room, and maybe one sitting with his hat on his knees in the lobby. All of them showing no interest in him, of course.

Until he'd crossed Clarence King's track. Or, more correctly, till Redeye had crossed his.

Raider had been lifting a few the evening before last in Talley's, a saloon on the northern fringe of town. The east wind, which never entirely ceased blowing down off the Plains, was moaning outside, making the doors and shut-

ters creak and bang. It was the reason the better homes
were built in the southern half of town, that wind. Granite
bluffs overlooked the passes east and west of town on the
south side, serving to break the force of the wind that
quested ceaselessly through the Moscas. So the better class
of houses were spared the buffeting the rest of the town
caught from the spring winds.

A heavyset man sauntered up to the bar beside Raider
and propped a hand-tooled boot on the brass rail.
"Whiskey," he ordered, in a gruff baritone. He looked up
at Raider and nodded, friendly-like. Raider nodded gravely
back. Alarm bells went off inside the Pink, and a warm
electric thrill surged through his belly.

"You new in these parts?" the stumpy man asked.

"Yep."

"Bartender!" the newcomer shouted. "Set my new pal
up with another of whatever he's drinkin'!"

It had seemed like just another frontier friendship—one
man cottoning to another for a drinking companion. It was
supposed to. Raider was not taken in for a moment. The
friendliness in Clarence King's red-rimmed hounddog eyes
never seemed to extend much past the lenses—and Raider
couldn't miss the heavy Colt hanging from Redeye's wide
waist, as it did from few others.

They'd extended inconsequentialities. Raider let on that
he'd been drifting from place to place, working at odd jobs
as the mood struck him. "Spent some time in Indian
territory," he said casually. "Thought I could use a change
of scenery, so I drifted down thisaways."

Redeye favored him with a wide, rubbery grin. "Had
enough of them squaws, hey? Dusky maidens can be fun,
but they tends to pall as a steady diet." He guffawed, but
there was a fresh look of appraisal in his eyes. Having
lately been in Indian territory wasn't enough to convict a
man of shady doings—at least, not in the eyes of the law.

But then, justice is blind, as the saying goes.

It would have been bad form—of a sort that was not
infrequently lethal—for Redeye to pry any further into the

stranger's past. So Redeye settled in to talk about himself.
He was a ranch hand, he said, in that gravelly drawl of his;
place in the mountains a few miles outside town, called the
Castile. "Owned by a Meskin fella, name of Durán,"
Redeye said. "Real straight-shooter."

Raider eyed his dress. His clothes were of better than
passable quality, if none too clean, from the sour smell
that hung about the man like a cloud. Beneath the overhang of his gut he had an expensive-looking silver belt
buckle inlaid with turquoise. King was obviously no dusty-
assed waddy, that much was clear. "You the foreman?"

"Naw." Redeye shook his head. "Just one o' the boys."
He paused a few beats, to make sure the slight emphasis
he'd given the word *boys* sunk in. "It's a real cushy bunk,
workin' for Mr. Durán."

They'd tipped a few more together and gone their sepa-
rate ways. Raider had not been surprised the next morning
to run into Redeye at Talley's again, and that evening
found himself in a friendly game of cards with Redeye and
a few more of the "boys": an apple-cheeked *nativo* named
David Apodaca; Claude Baker, a bluff balding man of
about Redeye's height and build with galluses stretched
almost to the breaking point across his expanse of belly; a
stocky man in his twenties, clean-shaven, with blond hair
and the heavy jaw and slit eyes of a pit bull. "This here's
Toby Sublette," Redeye said.

"You prob'ly heard of my people," he said, grinning
quickly with his thin-lipped mouth. It was a grin like the
shadow of a cloud passing along the ground—it came and
went fast and left no marks behind.

"Happens I have," Raider agreed. Milt Sublette and his
clan had been known as the most ruthless of all the fabled
Mountain Men, in their dealings with Indians and whites
alike. With an immense Bowie strapped to his hip—for
some reason Toby didn't carry a pistol as his partners
did—the young man looked like a logical inheritor of the
family tradition.

The game was friendly enough. Raider dropped a couple

of bucks in the opening hands, then started to win, and finished the evening almost a hundred dollars ahead of the game. It was an uncommon good-natured game. It may have been the basic human truth that a man of sense walks soft around a man with a weapon at his hip. But Raider thought it was something else.

They're actin' like it ain't their money they're losin', he told himself.

So he'd been sized up and, maybe, buttered up some too. All that remained was the offer. And it looked as if that was on its way.

They drank the whiskey down. Redeye raised his last glass, eyed it regretfully, then drank. "Well, I better mosey on back to the Castile," he said. "Why don't you come on back with me?"

The glass halted just shy of Raider's mouth. "What for?"

Redeye set his empty glass down and sat back in the chair, hitching his thumbs into his gunbelt. "Well, y'see, I mentioned runnin' into you to Mr. Durán, and he's allus lookin' for good hands, like. Asked if I might be able to git you to come on out and talk to him." He tipped his head sideways. "Less'n you got somethin' else on the fire."

"Never hurts to talk to a body," Raider said, deliberately noncommittal. He unfolded his lanky frame from the chair. "Let's ride."

"Whew." Judy Holiday sat down on a keg beside the wheel of the AOA wagon and mopped her forehead with a handkerchief, even though the afternoon sun was no more than pleasantly warm. "I think the South-Western Stage people are onto something. Things are not right in that town."

Doc was unloading crates of his Patented Egyptian Cure, in the little glass bottles with the colorful label he'd had printed up special in St. Louis. His coat was off and his vest unbuttoned. The sleeves of his white shirt were rolled up, to reveal forearms surprisingly thick and powerful for one of such a soft appearance. He set the crate he was toting on top of a stack of others and propped his rump on a corner of another. "What'd you find out?"

His pale blue eyes studied his co-operative with more than professional interest. In her neat little brown velvet suit, back in St. Louis, she'd been lovely in a cool, reserved way that matched her manner. On the train from St. Louis to Las Vegas, New Mexico Territory, where Doc had unloaded his wagon and Judith, his mule and inseparable companion, she had continued to dress and act with cool elegance.

But now . . . Doc didn't know whether it was the clothes she had assumed for her role, or the role itself, or maybe— just maybe—some well-hidden facet of Judy Holiday's character. But here, in the mellow afternoon sunlight, sitting on a molasses keg in a field to the west of town, Judy Holiday had a wild, wanton beauty that took Doc's breath away.

"I went into town to shop for notions and learn what I could, while you were negotiating with that Widow Whateley about letting us park the wagon in this field. People here are scared. The men won't meet your eye. And the women . . ." She shook her head. "Everyone looked at me when I first walked into town."

I have a good idea why, Doc thought, trying to keep from staring at her. *God, she looks fine in that blouse and skirt.*

"I thought they were just suspicious, at first. But do you know what, Doctor? They weren't accustomed to seeing a woman walking by herself. Especially not a young and—er, a young one."

Is she afraid to admit she's attractive, afraid of stirring my masculine passions? Doc wondered. *Or is she just being modest?*

"Did you manage to talk to anybody?"

"As I said, the menfolk wouldn't meet my eye. They were helpful enough at the general store, but they wouldn't talk. And the women weren't any too forthcoming. Until I met one of the Señora Hortensia's girls, taking her constitutional by the plaza.

" 'You just pulled in on that fancy medicine wagon, didn't you, honey?' she said.'' Doc raised an eyebrow. Judy Holiday's voice had taken on a higher pitch and a nasal West Texas twang he presumed were those of the soiled dove she'd conversed with. "I told her I had. 'Well, lemme tell you somethin', honey-chile,' she said. 'This town ain't like it seems. It ain't wise for a purty li'l gal like you to walk around by yourself, 'thout no bonnet to shade that face, nor a wrap o' some kind to cover up—' '' The operative broke off suddenly, reddening at the cheeks. "Anyway, she told me I should do the best I could to hide my appearance if I had to be out and about.

"We introduced ourselves. Her name was Amanada Susan Farthington, she claimed: 'Call me Mandy Sue.' She grew very serious. 'There's a man who runs this town,' she said. 'His boys swagger around like they was lords or somethin'—and they takes what they wants, if you take my meaning'.'

" 'You mean the mayor?' I asked, all innocence.

"She put back her head and laughed. She was really very pretty herself, with blond curls hanging past her shoulders, and a lace-trimmed blue parasol—of course, the roots of her hair were quite dark. 'Ain't you a caution, sweetie. No, hon, not the mayor. Somebody who, when he says jump, the mayor he just asks how high.'

" 'Naw, the man who runs this stinking burg is a Mexican man name of Durán. He lives up in the hills on a big ranch, with his crazy sister and his forty bullies. The Forty Thieves, ever'body calls 'em, after that old fairy tale that Danish or Dutch fella, Andersen, whatever—what he wrote.' ''

Doc laughed. He had several volumes of Burton's *The Thousand Nights and a Night* in the wagon, for late-night reading. The idea of Hans Christian Andersen writing the tales of Scheherazade was striking, to say the least.

Judy smiled and continued. " 'Aren't you afraid of them, Mandy Sue?' I asked. She just laughed.

" 'Sugah, those Forty Thieves wouldn't get too many kicks out of stealin' away the innocence of a gal like me. Hell, they even pay us, over to Señora Hortensia's, most of the time. But a girl like you . . .'

"She stopped, and turned to me, and looked me in the eye. 'I don't reckon most of the *respectable* women in town would give two cents for the difference between us. But there's a world o' difference all the same, for all that you ride around in that Gypsy wagon with that snake-oil peddler in the check suit. You're as innocent as a newborn babe. A body could read it in them emerald-green eyes of yours.' "

Doc noted that, now that Holiday was immersed in the role of Mandy Sue Farthington, she could repeat such appraisals of herself without self-consciousness. " 'So listen up, honey, and listen good,' she told me. 'You watch yourself from here on. Keep covered up. Stick close to your wagon at night. One of them Thieves takes a shine to you, honey, may God have mercy on you. 'Cause nobody's gonna lift a hand to help you.'

" 'Why doesn't the law do something?' I asked."

" 'Henry Durán is all the law there is in Las Peñas—him and that devil Abadón.' She stopped here, and shuddered. 'Now *that* one—well, he ain't hardly human. The things he does to a woman . . .'' She stopped, and her eyes blazed up. There were tears in them, too.

" 'Teresa, sweetie,' she said. 'If you see a big man, a Mexican, near seven feet tall with a face you'd only think to see in a nightmare and wearin' a machete strapped across his back, you keep clear of him, hear. 'Cause if he gets hold of you the best thing you could do is slice your wrists. The worst of the Apaches, Geronimo or Mountain Lion, they's kind compared to him.'

"About then a couple of men came into the plaza. I spotted them at once because they were both wearing guns. Hardly anyone does, in Las Peñas."

Doc nodded. It was a phenomenon he'd come across a lot, in the West and in the Deep South. A corrupt city government would outlaw the wearing of guns within the city limits—then deputize whole gangs of bullyboys to keep the populace in line at gunpoint. There were towns in the South where entire Klaverns of the Klan were sheriff's deputies. Durán's men—the Forty Thieves, were they? —may not have been official deputies, but they seemed to have official sanction for wearing weapons.

"Mandy Sue turned pale under her makeup. 'You run along now, honey-chile,' she said. 'Mind what I told you.' She walked over to intercept the two men and started to flirt with them—covering for me. I left as quickly as I could.''

"Good work," Doc murmured. He crossed his legs and knotted his hands over one knee. "You spend an hour in town, and you get a good picture of the lay of the land."

Judy dropped her eyes. Was she *blushing*? "Thank you," she said quietly.

"What conclusions do you derive from your reconnaissance, Operative Holiday?"

She looked up, all firm professionalism again. "The suspicions of the South-Western Stage Company seem justified, at least to the extent that criminal activities are running unchecked in Las Peñas."

"You think this Durán and his Arabian Nights thugs might have killed Odelbert?"

Judy bit her lip. "Doctor, you should have seen the look on that woman's face. I know small-town prostitutes, Doctor; I've portrayed them in the past—though I was never called upon to, to take my portrayal to the logical conclusion. . . ." She faltered, but quickly recovered her poise. "She was scared, scared to death. And not much scares a woman such as that."

Doc gazed across the field. A stream ran across one corner of it, and Doc had parked the wagon near it. Judith stood with her head down, cropping the weeds that grew rank along its banks. The sun was halfway past the zenith. It would soon dip behind the pine-clad peaks to the west.

"Looks as if we've got our work cut out for us, cleaning up this town," he said.

Holiday looked surprised. "Surely we won't have to? We simply collect the evidence, then turn it over to the authorities. We're not just private citizens, after all; we're Pinkertons. Even the territorial government will have to act on our findings."

He looked at her. She had a solid reputation as a superb agent—resourceful, clever, and courageous. But she seemed to possess a certain naiveté, all the same.

"Maybe so," he said. "Maybe so." He scooted himself off the corner of the crate. "We'd best start setting up. The locals are going to expect a rip-roarer of a show after this afternoon's buildup."

She stood up and walked around the end of the wagon. He watched the sway of her hips as she walked. *I don't think any of the local yokels are any more eager to see her in action than I am.*

He shook himself. That wasn't a very professional way to think. But it was hard not to think that way, all the time.

"This is going to be a tough assignment, Judith," he said aloud. The mule raised her head, snorted, and went back to pulling up soft reeds by the roots.

CHAPTER FOUR

Knee to knee with his new pal Redeye King, Raider rode northwards out of Las Peñas, through boulder-dotted fields to a trail leading through a forest of ponderosa pine. Spring didn't make such a big difference in the pinewoods as it would in a broadleaf forest, of course, but the feel and smell of spring were noticeable just the same. Little purple and blue wildflowers stuck round heads above still-yellow grass in the clearings; birds and squirrels chased each other chittering in the tree limbs overhead. Fortunately it was too early in the season for deerflies, the "stinging flies" after whom long-suffering Spanish explorers had named these mountains back in the sixteenth century. Raider had a special hatred for the tiny bloodsuckers, with the brown patterned wings like small moths.

"How far is it to this here Castile spread?" Raider asked after they'd ridden half an hour. They were out of the trees now, descending across a broad yellow meadow bisected by a stream. A few dark humped shapes away in the distance looked to Raider to be grazing cattle, probably Herefords. New Mexican ranchers didn't go in much for the temperamental and dangerous Longhorns.

"Jes' keep your shirt on," Redeye advised. He was slouched comfortably in the high-cantled Mexican saddle on the back of his big paddlefoot yellow paint. The saddle and bridle sported fancy silver inlay, confirming Raider's impression that King was no typical down-at-heels cowboy.

He didn't seem inclined to say more than that, so Raider just rode along on his leggy bay and kept his own counsel.

They topped a gradual rise and looked out across a wide clear valley. On a hill in the middle of it stood a tall house. Raider blinked. It was not the standard mud-brick hacienda, a boxy one-story sprawl, nor was it the mid-western style frame structure favored by certain homesick immigrants, especially in the eastern half of the territory. Instead it was a great gleaming two-story structure, white-washed a white that would be painful to the eye in brighter sun—more like a castle than a ranch house. A steeply pitched roof of half-cylindrical red tiles crowned the lordly manor. A six-foot wall, stuccoed white like the house itself, surrounded the mansion, a long low wooden bunkhouse, several outbuildings, and a tiny chapel behind the main house. The compound in front of the house was a large courtyard shaded by weeping willows.

Raider let out a long low whistle. "This Durán's got hisself a reg'lar fortress out here in the hills."

"That's Mr. Durán," Redeye said, sharper than he'd spoken out before.

"What's this 'mister' business, anyhow?" Raider asked. "If'n you don't mind my askin'. But I ain't accustomed to a white man misterin' a Mex, if you know what I mean."

"I understand," Redeye said, soft-like. "But Mr. Durán ain't no ordinary Mexican. He's like one of them Spanish fellers, a grandee. And that sister of his . . ." He shook his head. "That's a raven-haired catamount that ever was. But they're quality, Raider, old buddy. He's 'mister' to me—and to you, too." He chuckled. "Jest a word to the wise."

"Hmm," Raider said.

They rode down from the ridge. Clumps of cattle dotted the dun landscape, from the silvery ribbon of a stream that ran along the shallow valley up to the treeline. Raider saw three or four horsemen off in the distance, keeping an eye on the cattle—or something. He studied the house as they approached. A wagon road led down from the head of the valley a half-mile or so away to the big double gate of the compound, large enough to pass a wagon. Raider guessed the track was a longer route from town. The manor looked more and more fortresslike as they got nearer. The wall was stoutly built, with unmistakable firing slits at intervals, and he guessed there were platforms at the corners for guards to stand on.

"Dur—er, Mr. Durán sure seems to like his privacy," he said.

Redeye laughed. "He sure does. This here house is built right. Built a long time ago by Mr. Durán's great-grandfather, back afore the Mexican War. Used to have plenty of Injun worries, what with the Kiowa and Comanch' still runnin' wild on the plains. Even old Mangas Coloradas and his Mimbreños used to range up this far, back in the old days. Them walls is a yard thick. You couldn't blast through 'em in a week with a howitzer."

"He's got good fields of fire out o' them upper windows, too," Raider remarked. "And no cover for a good four, five hundred yards. Nobody gonna surprise *him*."

Redeye laughed again. "You seem to know a thing or two, boy."

"Reckon I do."

"Good man. I knowed it from the first."

They rode through the front gate. A few men loitered in the yard, yarning in the shade of the imported willows. They nodded and called greetings to Redeye. The two men tethered their mounts to a hitch rack in the shade of a willow and walked over to the covered porch.

"Who's the long drink of water, Redeye?" asked an old man with a tight cap of curly white hair covered his square skull, who sat on a whitewashed *banco* jutting from the wall of the house onto the porch. He wore a red shirt and a pistol that looked to Raider to be an old caplock Colt rebored for cartridges.

"The name's Raider," Raider said.

"Mr. Durán wants to talk to him," Redeye explained. "This here's Curly Snow." He nodded to the older man.

"Pleased to meet you," Snow said. He was a trim party for his age, and his face had been tanned and cured like leather by years of sun and wind.

A skinny Mexican in a loose *campesino* shirt, jeans, and boots with peeling soles squatted beside one of the square posts that held up the roof of the porch, whetting a needle-slim dagger on a blue-gray Arkansas soapstone. "This here's Miguelito Díaz." The Mexican looked up and favored Raider with a gap-toothed grin. He had a sharp fox's chin, high cheekbones, and a bad case of the cross-eyes.

"*Buenos,*" he said.

Raider nodded curtly and followed Redeye onto the shaded porch and through the elaborately carved door. Inside, the house was cool and dark. The walls were whitewashed inside as well as out. Raider saw that Redeye hadn't exaggerated; the outside walls were three-feet thick, the interior ones perhaps half that. Wool rugs patterned geometrically in shades of gray, black, and brown were spread on a floor of smooth red brick. Redeye removed his hat, almost reverently. Raider did likewise.

He was in a wide foyer. To his right an open door gave into a long room with a massive wooden table running lengthwise, and heavy round beams, *vigas*, giving the impression of hanging just above the head of a tall man. Immediately before him a stairway curved up to a gallery on the second story that spanned the foyer from side to side. The banister and the gallery's balustrade were carved of some striped maple, a wood not native to this part of the country; Raider figured it must have cost a fortune to freight across the Great Plains or the Llano Estacado.

A huge oil portrait in a gilded, ancient frame as broad as Raider's hand hung beside the stairway. A rail-thin party with a snowy goatee, thin mustache, and hair swept back from a high narrow skull stood glowering through a fine network of cracks at the highly polished treads and risers of the staircase. He was dressed in old-timey splendor, in black velvet with white ruffles at neck and wrists. A broad gold strap crossed his chest diagonally, and from it a gold-hilted rapier hung by his hip. A Spaniard, by the look of him, dark-complected with sharp-sculpted features. But his eyes didn't look Spanish to Raider. They barely looked human: wolf's eyes, an eerie yellow-gray.

"Don Rodrigo," Redeye whispered. "A ancestor of Mr. Durán's. Come over from Spain with ol' Cortéz hisse'f."

An Indian woman, tiny and wrinkled, appeared from the rear of the house. Busy sounds came from that direction, as though folk were working in the kitchen somewhere back thataway. "Excilda, go tell Mr. Durán I brung the feller he wanted to see." The woman nodded silently and moved off through the door that opened to their left, at the foot of the wide stairway.

Now that they were in the keep itself a fit of nervousness had come over Redeye. He fidgeted, shifting his weight from foot to foot, twisting the brim of his Stetson in his hands and flashing convictionless grins at Raider, as if trying to reassure the newcomer. "You'll like Mr. Durán." He was whispering now. "He's a real man, real macho."

"Who's that? Enrico?" The voice floated down the stairs like a cloud of exotic fragrance, low and thrilling and feminine in a way that touched Raider in the pit of his belly. *What we got here*? he wondered. He rolled his weight onto the balls of his feet and waited like a boxer for the bell.

With a click-click of steel heel-taps a woman descended into view from the gallery above. "*Enrico*—oh." She stopped and stared down at the two.

She was a tall woman, not many inches shorter than Raider. A slender figure, with high breasts, small and sharp, and fine lean legs, was encased in white blouse and tight gray riding breeches. Tight black boots, polished so brightly that Raider reckoned he could've shaved in them with little danger to his face, reached to her knees. Black hair was piled in a lustrous knot atop her head. Her face was coldly lovely, olive-skinned and fine-boned, with a narrow aquiline nose. Raider couldn't miss the resemblance between the woman's face and that of the stern white-haired black-clad man in the portrait. With a cool thrill he noted her eyes were the same as well—yellow and feral.

And maybe just a little mad.

Instinctively, Raider reached up and preened his black bandit's mustache. "Good afternoon, ma'am," he said.

Her eyes met his. For a moment he thought he'd made a mistake. They were as cold as a snake's. "Who's this, Clarence?" she asked, holding the Pinkerton's gaze with her own.

"Why, this is Mr. Raider, señorita. New feller in town. He—uh, your brother wanted to see him."

"I see." She descended the remaining steps in a gliding walk. Maybe he was too stricken with her strange beauty to hear straight, but Raider could have sworn she made no noise.

She stopped a few feet in front of him and extended a languid hand. He took it, bowed over it, and kissed it, a gesture he'd learned from Doc. Señorita Durán, as Raider took her to be, smiled with her thin exquisite lips. *Bless the little bastard*, he thought. He swore to himself not to hit his partner, next time he took a mind to.

"Welcome, Mr. Raider," she said in her husky voice. "I am Dama Sancha, sister to the master of this house. I trust that you will forgive it that this cur lacked grace to introduce me."

Redeye turned ash-white. "*De nada*," Raider made haste to reply in his fluent Spanish. "It is nothing. Your beauty and grace leave me no room to think of such things." Amazing, how he could rattle of so easily in Spanish things he wouldn't be caught dead saying in English, even if he could think of them. Funny language, Spanish.

She laughed. Her teeth were even and very white. "You are most courteous, sir. And you speak our tongue most elegantly. I would like—"

"Clarence?" A man's voice called, before Sancha could finish the tantalizing wisp of sentence. A wave of irritation crossed the woman's face.

A heartbeat later a man appeared in the door to the left. "There you are, Clarence," he said. He nodded shortly to the woman. *"Buenas tardes."*

She nodded formally back. "Enrico."

He turned to the stranger, raising a brow in inquiry. Still stinging from Sancha's rebuke, the perspiring Redeye said quickly, "Here he is, Mr. Durán. The man you wanted to see. Mr. Raider."

Henry Durán thrust out his hand. "I'm pleased to meet you," he said in a rich, well-modulated baritone. He was a small man, compact. His handshake, warm and dry, gave the impression of wiry strength. The way he held himself, poised and taut as a greyhound, bespoke restless, nervous energy.

"Pleasure's mine."

"I see you've met my sister." A shadow crossed his face. It was a fine face, handsome, but marred by a liberal spattering of pockmarks, legacy of some childhood disease. His hair was as black and shiny as an Indian's, and his eyes were those of his sister, and of Don Rodrigo Durán. "She is a great help to me, running the hacienda."

"My brother is too kind," Sancha said, in a tone that scraped down Raider's vertebrae. He hoped he wasn't about to be caught in some kind of crossfire between the lynx-eyed siblings.

"If you will excuse us, Sancha, Mr. Raider and I have certain matters to discuss."

"Of course. I would not dream of interfering in men's business." She held out her hand to Raider. "I hope we will meet again soon," she said in Spanish.

After the briefest hesitation Raider took her hand and lifted it once again to his lips. "No more than I," he wanted to say. But somehow he couldn't, with Henry Durán's eyes on him. He kissed her hand without speaking and released it. Was that a cool smile of content that played on her lips before she turned away?

Durán put a hand on his shoulder and steered him back through the door from which he'd emerged. "Come with me, my friend. There's a place where we can talk.'' He led him down a corridor with dark wooden doors on either side, and into a door on the left, at the very end of the hallway. Redeye trotted at their heels.

Inside was a desk and several wooden chairs. The room was in a corner of the big house, and windows in two adjoining walls gave good light. ''Be seated,'' Durán said, going to a tall beautifully carved hutch. ''Would you care for a drink?''

''Whiskey.'' Raider folded himself into a chair.

He looked around the small room as Durán poured two glasses full of amber liquid. The walls were lined with shelves. Most of these were crammed with books, with age-blackened, cracking spines and gold lettering in Spanish and English. But these weren't what caught Raider's eye. It was the odd assortment of objects ranged on the shelves. Not the usual run of Victorian bric-a-brac—not at all.

Durán handed Raider a glass, then took his own behind the desk and sat down, leaving Redeye to pour his own drink. ''You like my collection, señor?''

''It's differ'nt.''

It was indeed. Fragments of bone, pottery, carvings in stone. Flint arrowheads affixed to a black velvet-covered board. Ceramic shards crossed by bands of black and beige. Tiny figurines and a chunk of wall-carving in some sort of yellow limestone. One in particular caught Raider's eye, an image or idol almost a foot tall, carved in some black jade. It represented what seemed to be a man in outlandish armor, with a towering feathered headdress, holding an oddly shaped shield and a sort of a toothed club. ''You have discriminating tastes, Mr. Raider,'' Durán said, noting where his gaze had fallen. ''That is the prize of my collection. A representation of Tezcatlipoca, foremost of all the Aztec gods. A cruel god, Creator and Destroyer both—a splendid ambivalence, *qué no*?''

He sipped his drink. ''I have many relics of the past of this ancient, wild country. See here.'' He pulled open a door of the heavy desk—which looked rather ancient to Raider itself—rummaged around, and laid something reverently on the green baize blotter before him, inviting his guest's scrutiny.

It was a broad spearhead of yellow-gray flint, four or five inches long, with a blunt-angled point and a notched rear. Raider picked it up and examined it. Even his unpracticed eye could tell it was finely worked. A wide shallow groove ran from the rear most of the way to the tip. He shrugged, made a mouth, and laid it back down.

"Ancient men made that point, an immeasurably long time ago," Durán said. His yellow eyes glowed. "*Indios*, perhaps, or a folk who dwelt here earlier even than they. I dug it up myself, near Capulín Mountain. I feel it may be a vital piece of the story of our kind."

He sighed and restored the artifact to its place in the drawer. "But I perceive that archaeology holds little interest for you, Mr. Raider. A pity."

Raider sipped his drink and said nothing.

Durán gazed out one window. Raider took the opportunity to study him further. He was dressed in a white shirt, black vest, black trousers, and cowboy boots, all obviously expensive. For all the simplicity of his garb he exuded the same dignity and elegance as his forebearer in the old portrait. Here in his castle he wore no weapon, though Raider didn't doubt for a moment he could handle one—any kind, you name it—as well as most men. He had that air of competence, of total self-assurance.

"You wanted to see me."

Durán turned his head back. "Yes. My men have been keeping an eye on you, since you arrived in Las Peñas."

Raider took a sip. The whiskey was mellow, smoky, and good. "I noticed."

Durán's eyetooth showed in a quick smile. "So they were clumsy." His eyes promised the ones at fault would be dealt with.

"Not really. Man rides a narrow trail long as I have, he sorta starts to git a second sense for that kinda thing."

"What sort of trail have you ridden, Mr. Raider? What men call a crooked one, perhaps?"

It was plain arrogance to ask a question like that, in the heart of his stronghold. "What's it to you?" Raider shot back.

Redeye tensed. Durán laughed at Raider's calculated rudeness. "I won't fence with you any more, sir. I run the town of Las Peñas—I, and no other. I do so through a band of strong, hard men whom it pleases the vulgar to call the Forty Thieves." He smiled. "It has rather a ring to it, that name, does it not?"

Raider said nothing.

"You've been watched, as I said. I know what you are: a gun for hire." He leaned forward with his elbows on the desk and steepled his fingers. "I want to hire you."

"See, Rade, buddy?" A beam of relief split Redeye's face. "I tol' you you was a good man. I told Mr. Durán here, too."

"What do you offer?"

Durán sat back. "I'll pay you a good salary. Sixty dollars a month, say." It was twice the going salary for a cowhand. "But that's only part of it. I am engaged in a number of . . . enterprises. According to your participation in these you will receive a percentage of the proceeds.

"But more than that: the power. You've spent a week in Las Peñas. You've seen the way people look when my men walk through the streets. They cower in fear." He licked thin lips. "They know that everything they own, their property, their women—even their *lives*—are held on sufferance. What my men want, they take!" He made a grabbing motion in the air. "And none dare refuse. So it is in Las Peñas. My private fief. And soon—who knows?" He shrugged. "This is a large territory. There is room for ambition."

Redeye was leaning forward, hands on knees, eyes and lips glistening. "So, Señor Raider," Durán said. "Are you with us."

Raider drank again. "No."

Stunned silence came crashing down. "*Perdone*?" Durán asked, as if unwilling to believe his ears.

"Thank you kindly, Mr. Durán. But I ain't interested." He stood up.

The rancher stared at him, his face bleak as a skull. Redeye bounced to his feet, knocking his chair clattering to the brick floor. "Are you crazy?"

"Nope. Just not int'rested."

He started to turn. Redeye grabbed his sleeve. "But Raider! You said—"

"I said I'd come talk to Mr. Durán. I done so. Now I'm goin' back to town."

"But Rade! He—he offered you a *job*!"

"I'm right flattered," Raider said, more to Durán than the fear-faced man at his elbow. "But I reckon on workin' my own angle, thank you just the same."

Durán smiled thinly. "Las Peñas is not a rich town, señor," he said. "There is not much left over for the—how do you say it?—the free lance."

"I'll take my chances."

Redeye had gone gray, and his face was slack with terror. "You don't know the chances you're *takin'*, boy."

"Henry?" a feminine voice spoke from the doorway. This one was high-pitched, light and lacy.

Raider turned his head. A blond woman stood in the doorway. "Oh!" she said, putting a hand to full red lips whose color was owed to art and nature both. "I hope I'm not interruptin' anything."

"Not at all, Sallee, my dear," Duran said stiffly. He rose. "The gentleman was just leaving."

Her eyes ran down Raider's long frame. "Oh, that's a shame," she said.

Durán frowned. Raider was inclined to agree with Sallee. He wouldn't mind taking some time to get to know this one. She didn't come up past his breastbone, but she packed a lot into a short space. Her hair was pale gold, piled up on top with long curls hanging to either side of a face that was round, pert, and lovely. Her eyes were wide and blue, her nose slightly retroussé. She wore a green silk dress cut sufficiently low in front that Raider had no doubt the remarkable jut of her breasts was all natural, with no help from art at all. Her waist was narrow, her hips full. The fullness of her skirts let Raider see nothing of the shape of her legs, but what he could see indicated they'd definitely reward closer study.

"My name's Raider," he said. "I'm right pleased to meet you."

"Oh, the pleasure's mine," the woman cooed. "I'm Sallee LaSalle."

"Sallee," Durán said sharply. She looked at him, then up at Raider in consternation.

"Like the man said," Raider said, "I was just leavin'. Good day, Miss LaSalle."

"You're sure you won't reconsider, Mr. Raider?" Durán asked tautly.

"Yep." He put his black Stetson on. "*Adiós.*"

Durán stood. "*Hasta luego*," he said. *See you soon.* Raider frowned and left.

Redeye pelted after him. "For God's sake, Rade! You can't mean it."

"Happens I do. I told you. I ride alone."

His long strides left the man standing, panting for breath. "But he'll kill you!" he shouted after Raider's retreating back. From the edge of panic in his voice, raw and ugly as a running sore, it was clear that Clarence Redeye King feared his esteemed employer might have the same fate in mind for him. Raider ignored him. He strode into the foyer and turned right to the front door.

The men in the yard outside were looking at him with flat gazes. He immediately sensed hostility. Had Durán called to them out the window? Or had some expected signal not been given? Whatever the case was, this was the tricky part of Raider's plan: riding out of the courtyard alive.

He felt the eyes following him as he walked across the ten yards of packed tan caliche that separated the doorway from the rack where his bay was hitched. The horse bobbed its head, snorted, and rolled its eyes. It could sense the ugliness, and was afraid. So was Raider, but he kept it from showing with an iron will.

He started to unhitch the horse. Something flashed past his head. He ducked his head frantically aside as it thwacked into the bole of the willow. It was one of Miguelito's daggers sticking in the soft gray-green bark, giving off a musical hum as it vibrated.

Raider looked around. Díaz was still squatting on the porch. He grinned, displaying the gap between his front teeth. "*Mil perdones, señor,*" he said. He had the nasal accent of the Mexican countryside. "I thought I see a horsefly landing on the tree, there by your head."

The men in the yard laughed uproariously. Raider grinned sourly, seemed to shrug—

And a yard-long flame lanced from the pistol that appeared as if by magic in his left hand. Miguelito screamed shrilly as the .44-.40 ball smashed the heel off his right boot. He went sprawling on the tile of the porch.

"Funny," Raider drawled as he holstered his piece. "Coulda swore there was a sidewinder there, right next your foot."

In deadly stillness he swung aboard the bay and went trotting out the gate.

CHAPTER FIVE

Yellow lamplight danced on the tent walls and the eager faces of the audience. "Welcome," the man in the midnight-blue turban intoned. The glow from the kerosene lanterns hung from the posts that upheld the canvas roof reflected off the polished top surface of the podium in front of him, giving his face a demonic underlighting. "Tonight you, the citizens of the fair city of Las Peñas, will experience something that goes far beyond what you have ever known before. You will look—with your own eyes!—across immeasurable gulfs of time and space. Behold the secrets of the ancients—view at first hand the building of the Pyramids and the interment of a Royal Mummy in its tomb of barbaric splendor and imperial pretense! Learn the secret of the mysterious origin of the Patented Egyptian Cure, sovereign specific for every ailment of body and mind, which will be made available in limited quantity tonight to a fortunate few! See Madame Teresa, lineal descendant of the Pharaohs of Egypt, risk her life and lovely limbs in handling a fearsome Serpent in the awesome Dance of the Python!"

The audience sat up a little straighter on their benches at the mention of Madame Teresa and her serpent dance. "I heard she does it nekkid," someone whispered hoarsely from the rear of the tent, adding, "With nary a stitch of clothin'!" rather unnecessarily.

Doc pressed his hands together before his face and

bowed his head slightly to hide his grin as someone angrily shushed the whisperer. He had bribed several urchins that afternoon to spread that selfsame rumor. *Always gratifying to know one has invested wisely*, he reflected.

A large tent had been erected next to the AOA wagon, using the wagon itself for one wall. A number of benches were set facing a low wooden platform, on which stood a pedestal, apparently of marble but actually of cunningly painted papier-mâché, which served as Doc's podium. Behind Doc—who looked very mysterious in white shirt and black pants, with purple silk cummerbund and a cloak to match his indigo headcloth—a broad canvas scrim stretched along the hull of the wagon, bearing the same painting of camels, palm trees, and pyramids featured on the labels of the Egyptian Cure, much enlarged. Midnight blue bunting, scattered with gold stars, framed the picture.

A good fifty of the residents of Las Peñas and environs were crammed into the tent, jam-packed onto the benches and standing in the aisle and around the walls. They stood or sat with the tension of eager anticipation, champing lustily at bags of peanuts and popcorn that they'd bought at Eloy Martínez's General Store before trooping out to the Widow Whateley's boulder-scattered field. It was a good audience, hungry for excitement and none too sophisticated.

"Allow me to introduce myself. I am commonly known as Dr. Weatherbee, a humble man of medicine. But for tonight, let me stand revealed to you by my mystical name: Al Tabib, the Healer, in the language of the far-off land of Egypt. My assistant—"

He paused. The audience drew in a collective breath. The tent flap behind Doc and to his right parted noiselessly and a figure glided in. The crowd let its breath out in a sigh of disappointment. The much-heralded figure, face, and hair of Madame Teresa were muffled in a black cowled cloak that covered her from head to foot.

"My assistant, Madame Teresa, herself a skilled student of the occult arts."

She bowed, her hands clasped before her. Her face was

lost in the shadow of her hood. "Shuck on outa that robe, sweetie, and let's get a look at you!" somebody yelled.

"Shet up, Clem, or you'll be lookin' at a handful of yer own damn teeth," somebody shouted back in an impressive bass. In the hubbub "Madame Teresa" withdrew as silently as she had come.

Doc drew a gold-tipped black wand from his sleeve and tapped it against the copper plate atop his podium. "I must ask that you refrain from demonstrations as much as possible," he said gravely, "though I know that as tonight's mysteries are unveiled it would prove beyond human endurance to utterly suppress your spontaneous expressions of wonder. But we are dealing with ancient forces here, arcane powers. Only my great wisdom holds these forces in check. If my concentration is disturbed . . . I cannot answer for the consequences."

A satisfactory thrill of horror passed visibly through his audience. "Now," he said, raising his head and declaiming. "I present to you—the Nile Valley." The scene behind him began to move to his right, to be replaced by a picture of a broad river, far bluer than the actual Nile could ever hope to be, flowing through a lushly green valley. On either side of the valley rose sand dunes, stark and barren. "An oasis of plenty in the inhospitable desert of ancient Egypt. Great was the wealth of its Pharaoh—"

The scene moved on to show a king with a protuberant false beard and a cobra-crowned headdress sitting on his throne, being fanned by scantily clad slave girls while bald scribes knelt before him, presenting scrolls for his approval.

"—and wise were his counselors. He asked of them, 'How shall I cheat death, that comes to kings as it does to the lowest commoner, yea, the lowest slave?' And they answered, 'Build for yourself the mightiest of tombs, O Pharaoh.'"

The scene scrolled on to a picture of gangs of slaves straining under the lash to draw gigantic stone blocks in the full force of the sun's heat. It moved quite smoothly and stopped exactly where it should, with the picture well centered, as Doc confirmed by sneaking a quick glance over his shoulder. Judy Holiday was doing her job with commendable skill. In this case her job was to turn the vertical spool that took up the long strip of canvas on which a St. Louis artist had painted—at considerable personal expense to Doc—a series of scenes of life in ancient Egypt. It wasn't an extraordinarily stunning effect, but the yokels seemed taken with it.

The scene rolled on, to the accompaniment of Doc's lecture, showing the pyramids rising to completion, the death of the Pharaoh, and his embalming—this with the most tasteful Victorian circumspection; he didn't want the onlookers regurgitating their peanuts and forty-rod down the backs of one another's necks from too much realism— and his entombment in a splendid golden mummy case. "Lying in his golden repose, the Pharaoh achieved immortality indeed, of a sort. For he has come down to us in this distant age, perfectly preserved. What accomplished this miracle? What kept the great Khufu's mortal remains safe against the ravages of eons? The Egyptian mages employed in his embalming a potation that had already proved itself efficacious in extending life. For generations the secret of this miraculous elixir was passed down from father to son, long forgotten outside of a family of Egyptian sages, until it was revealed to me, Al Tabib, who now makes it available to the suffering multitudes as Doctor Weatherbee's Patented Egyptian Cure, available at a dollar a bottle."

At this point a chinless hayseed with ears like jug handles, sitting in the very front row, lolled his pointy head back on his pencil neck. His mouth hung open and emitted a fearsome snore that sounded like a ripsaw digging into a redwood slab. Doc flung out his hand. A ball of fire leapt from his fingertips, straight for the offender's face. It vanished a scant half inch from the tip of the man's nose. He opened his eyes, let out a squall of terror, and fell over backwards.

As the spectators behind helped him back onto the

bench to the accompaniment of general hilarity, Doc made sure another pill of thin paper impregnated with nitric and sulfuric acid flash solution was handy for palming. He found the stuff a great aid to the healer's art.

The end of the panorama was usually a dangerous spot. The audience got restive and fidgeted in their seats, and if anyone was minded to heckle, this was when they usually started warming up their pipes. The dozer had provided a nice diversion and livened things up enough that Doc drew out the spiel on the virtues of his Egyptian Cure that he usually delivered at this point. *After all, I've got to pay for the damned panorama.*

Then, as a thin, eerie piping rose from somewhere behind him, he launched into a routine of stage conjuring, which he loved. He produced flamboyant fans and cascades of cards, divined the identities of cards chosen by members of the audience, prophesied which card they would pick, amazing all with his unerring accuracy. He produced colorful silk scarves from thin air, made them change color, tied them together and made the knots mysteriously dissolve with a flick of his wrist, then made the scarves vanish. He linked and unlinked rings. All the while he kept up a running patter that connected all this fanfaronade with Egyptian mysticism, quite ingeniously. He was no Robert Houdini, but he had reason to be proud of his accomplishment at sleight-of-hand.

The cowled Teresa appeared bearing a golden bowl, cleverly designed so as not to bear a fatal resemblance to either a thundermug or a spittoon. "Behold!" he cried. "A white dove, sacred to Isis, goddess of fertility and the Moon!" His hand brought forth a fluttering white bird, while the onlookers cried out in wonder and delight.

"Now," he said, hurriedly handing the flapping dove to Madame Teresa before it committed an indignity on his sleeve, "some of you may suspect my motives in bringing you the benefits of ancient wisdom in the form of my Patented Egyptian Cure. No—do not deny it. You would be other than human if you could altogether refrain from speculating that my motives may be purely pecuniary.''

Teresa had vanished with the bird. Doc picked up the bowl. ''I have no need of earthly gain,'' he announced, ''for when I wish it, my bowl overflows with coins.''

''Naw!'' somebody hollered.

He turned the bowl this way and that. ''Behold! See that the bowl is innocent of content.'' The spectators nodded and whispered to one another. *Yup, it's empty, anybody can see that.* ''And when I require funds—'' his right hand suddenly darted out like a frog's tongue, —''I pluck them from the air!''

He flung something into the bowl with a ringing clang. The audience gasped. He set the bowl upon the podium, reached inside, and with great deliberation drew forth a gleaming silver dollar.

Applause burst forth like a mountain cloudburst.

He quickly drew several more coins from the air before him. ''And not only do I find money in the very air''—he stepped from behind the podium and into the aisle between the front two benches—''I find money everywhere I look.'' And he removed a gleaming coin from the white bun of hair belonging to an elderly *nativa* in a black dress and shawl, who cackled in delight.

He proceeded to make coins appear from a number of unlikely places, lanterns, tentpoles, hair, ears, and in the case of one prodigiously endowed man, a nose. When he was finished with the routine, which was about the same age as the pyramids once more portrayed on the backdrop, he had the audience eating out of his hand.

''And now,'' he said, returning to the stage, ''I relinquish your attention in favor of my lovely assistant, Madame Teresa. She is the last survivor of the ancient royal family of Egypt. In her veins runs the blood of those who raised the Pyramids—and of the lovely Cleopatra! She will perform for you a ritual dance of Cyclopean antiquity.'' He raised a hand. ''Let me caution you! If you are faint of heart, I beg of you to forgo the pleasure of witnessing the dance, for it entails the Princess placing herself in mortal danger! And now—Teresa, Princess of Ancient Egypt!''

As he spoke, Judy Holiday had emerged from the wings, still wearing her enigmatic cloak. Now she flung it open and let it fall. Stunned silence filled the tent.

Her auburn hair was tied in an elaborate knot, bound with gold wire. A ruby gleamed in the center of her forehead. From beneath it her eyes burned like green beacons above a gauzy veil that covered without concealing the lower part of her face. She wore a cloth-of-gold vest encrusted in jewels, and a long-sleeved blouse and baggy pantaloons of the same half-transparent stuff as her veil. Beneath these she wore the merest halter and a sort of loincloth, which seemed to consist entirely of gold coins somehow linked together. Another ruby gleamed from her navel. Her figure was everything her appearance in the wagon box that day had hinted—and more. Gazing on her, Doc found himself having as much trouble drawing breath as the no-longer-somnolent rube in the front row.

The single eyebrow of a stern matron sitting toward the rear knotted in righteous rage. The nerve of that Jezebel, to uncover herself so in public! She pointed a brawny arm and opened her mouth to denounce this wickedness.

What came out was a strangled scream.

The discarded cloak had begun to stir. A head, wedge-shaped and blunt-nosed, poked out of it, and then a long sinuous body began to slither forth from its folds. ''Behold the deadly serpent,'' Doc intoned, in a doomful voice. ''The dreaded Python, messenger of Set, Egyptian God of Evil.''

''Oh!'' cried the ax-faced matron in melting horror. ''The poor child! Won't someone help her?''

''Beware, ladies and gentlemen! I must urgently advise you to keep to your seats. The embrace of this creature can crush the life from the strongest man in seconds!''

Teresa had turned to face the loathsome creature. It had crept free of the robe and now lay revealed, fully six feet of muscular body, pale brown, with a dark streak marked with pale ovals along its back, and brown patches with light centers along its scaled sides. Its belly was yellow. "The Princess observes the monster," Doc said. "Fearless is her gaze; fearlessly she moves forward to grapple it." Teresa stepped forward, lunged, came up with the snake twining about her slender forearms.

Women screamed and hid their eyes. Strong men blanched. "Now, look on the struggle between the bright Princess and the messenger of Darkness! On its outcome hangs the fate of the world!"

From a stand behind his podium Doc took a violin and bow, tucked the instrument beneath his chin, and began to play a wild discordant air. Teresa began to writhe, as the serpent lashed its reddish tail. *Poor Sam!* Doc thought. The boa constrictor was of course totally harmless to anyone who didn't happen to be a rodent—though Doc suspected there were one or two of his onlookers who might have something to fear from the serpent, at that. At the moment the only thought in its dim brain was to escape from its keeper and friend Judy, who had inexplicably chosen to attack it. Judy's skillful acting made Sam's frantic twinings and thrashings appear to be a horrid assault on her.

A droning tone came plangently from the violin. Teresa went to her knees as the monstrous serpent wrapped itself around her shoulders. Her lissome body swayed this way and that as she wrestled with the creature. Fear for her safety began to have a marked competitor in the minds of the masculine onlookers. The Princess bent back and back, small hands clutching feebly at the relentless coils of the snake. "Oh, the poor brave girl!" A woman's sob rose above the tumult of frightened voices.

Suddenly the violin's sound soared. The woman's body snapped forward. The snake flailed mightily, but the tide of battle had turned. Princess Teresa began to pry its coils from her fair form as the music wailed toward a crescendo.

Doc played madly and expertly, hugely enjoying himself. He was a good showman, but he had to admit the female

Pinkerton was as good a performer as any he'd laid eyes on. If she had the least fear of the snake, Doc had never noticed it—she actually seemed to *like* the creature. Yet her death duel with the poor unassuming snake was so convincing even Doc felt a tingle of concern.

Loop by loop the Princess freed herself. The violin's skirl stopped. Teresa tore the snake from her, then held her vanquished foe above her head.

Applause beat over her like breakers on a lee shore. Everyone in the house was busy shouting him or herself hoarse, and there were more than a few moist eyes. Teresa knelt before them a moment, soaking up their adulation and admiration, then ran offstage to get some warm clothes for herself and a field mouse for the thoroughly terrified Sam.

Doc stood where he was, violin stuck under his chin, bow poised. He should have given her a fanfare as she left, but he stood as if frozen.

Three men stood at the back of the tent. He had not noticed them come in, but he would have sworn they hadn't been there during his lecture or conjuring act. All three of them wore pistol belts: the tall, skinny towheaded youth to the left; the elegantly slim Mexican in a black sack coat, string tie, and flat-brimmed Stetson on the right; and the giant who loomed like an Egyptian idol from the panorama in the center.

His face was massive in size and ugliness, resembling a granite mask by a sculptor either clumsy or immaculately, subtly skilled. He stood with his thumbs in the pockets of his jeans, feet wide apart. The hilt of a machete stuck out above his right shoulder. His eyes were small and glittering—and they followed Judy Holiday with unhealthy closeness as she completed her dance and ran from the tent.

Seven feet tall with a face you'd only think to see in a nightmare and wearin' a machete strapped across his back. The words of the whore Mandy Sue rang in Doc's brain as the audience leapt to its feet in an exuberant ovation.

The man at the back of the tent may not have been seven feet tall, but he came closer than most. And his face . . . Doc didn't have many nightmares that bad, imaginative cuss though he was.

I might after this job, he thought. A cold shiver of premonition ran down his back on centipede legs.

The giant turned and was gone. His comrades followed him into the night. Doc shook himself, trying to free himself of the dread that gripped him. "Thank you very much, ladies and gentlemen," he heard himself say. "If you will be patient a few moments more, the lovely Princess Teresa will return, bearing bottles of Doctor Weatherbee's Egyptian Cure, Elixir of the Ages!"

"A fabulous job, Operative Holiday," Doc enthused. "You were incredible. Like something out of a—ugh!—a dream." With a grunt of effort he hefted a case of Egyptian Cure back into the bed of the wagon. It had been a successful evening. He had sold out three whole cases of the stuff.

"You really think so, Doctor?" Judy stood with her cloak around her against the chill, unfastening the ties that held the canvas tent to the wagon frame. Her eyes shone in the light of a kerosene lamp slung to the rear of the Studebaker.

"I do." He dusted his hands against each other and eyed the tent. It was going to be a bitch to break down, even with Judy's strong and capable hands to help—the rigors of life on the road brooked no nonsense about preserving a woman from hard physical work, not that Judy seemed to mind pitching in, any more than she seemed to mind disporting her beautiful body beneath the lustful gazes of a lot of hayseeds and Mexicans. They couldn't risk leaving the tent up overnight, not the way the damned wind was up here. The canvas was cracking and booming like an artillery duel as it was. "You're a constant source of amazement to me, Ju—er, Miss Holiday."

"Oh, you don't—" She stopped suddenly. Her eyes stared past him.

Doc turned, suddenly painfully aware that his shoulder rig was stowed away inside the wagon with his regular clothes. A figure loomed out of the darkness, a moving colossus, with two human-sized attendants following behind. "*Buenos noches*," the giant rumbled, his voice like a rockslide in progress.

"Good evening," Doc said, forcing himself to sound casual. "May I help you gentlemen?"

"I am Marcosio Abadón," the giant announced. Doc felt his heart skip a beat. "These are my good friends Joselito Chacón"—the shorter Mexican flashed a quick smile beneath his thin mustache—"and Mr. Slowhand McVie." The towheaded boy bared his teeth in a slow grin and gave Judy a sly sidelong glance.

You fool! Doc told himself bitterly. *Getting caught without a weapon in reach!* There were not as many men who could best him in barehand rough and tumble as one might think to look at him—Rade was one, drat him—but he knew that he had no prayer of coping with this monster. He might consider going up against Abadón with a Sharps Big .50 rifle in hand—or better yet, a Gatling gun.

"Right enjoyed your show, ma'am," the blond kid told Judy. He still couldn't bring himself to look her in the eye.

"Thank you," she said. Her undefinable exotic accent was impeccably in place. *Good girl!* Doc thought.

"I'm sorry, gentlemen, but I have packed away all that remained of my Egyptian Cure. If you wish to come back tomorrow night, I could perhaps reserve you a bottle or two."

"We ain't interested in your colored water, señor," Chacón said with a sneer. He let the expression slip into a leer directed at Judy.

Abadón swiveled his gigantic head and gave the dapper man a look of mild reproach. Chacón's olive face went pale and he quickly dropped his eyes. "Forgive my *carnal*," he said ponderously. "He don't mean to be rude. We come to talk business with you, Doctor."

Doc saw a muscle tighten at the corner of Chacón's lean jaw. *Carnal* meant brother, literally—but it was usually used to denote a hillbilly, a country cousin with shit on his feet and under his fingernails. That the aristocratic Chacón didn't drill a .45-caliber hole through Abadón's pendulous belly scared Doc more than anything else about the giant had.

Both the sharply dressed Mexican and his taller blond friend with the black gloves and the blue scarf knotted at his throat were showing two guns apiece. A man didn't do that unless he was either a damn fool or a damned hot shot; even Raider, who handled a pistol with the grace and skill with which Doc manipulated the coins he used in his Shower of Wealth routine, normally wore just one. These two looked distressingly competent. Abadón obviously outranked his pals. But Doc had met few Mexicans who were slaves to authority, and none who weren't on a hair trigger where their personal honor was concerned. The only reason the giant could make a crack like that about his comrade and live had to be that Chacón was mortally afraid of him.

"It's rather late," Doc pointed out. The stars glittered coldly overhead. The wind sobbed like a lost soul through the mountains.

"Our business, she won' take long, señor. All you have to do is pay us a little *dinero*, a little cut of your take, and *mira*! we go away and leave you in peace."

Doc blinked owlishly. "But I don't understand. I spoke to the mayor today, and he said nothing about any fees."

Slowhand laughed. "Ain't the mayor who we're collectin' for. It's Durán."

"*Señor* Durán," Abadón corrected. McVie just shrugged. *He's either crazy, brave or stupid, that one,* Doc thought. "*Señor* Durán, he is the *patrón* of Las Peñas. He asks the contribution. Just a small share of your great income, eh?" He smiled. His teeth were perfect. It added to his menace.

Oh, God, here it comes. Doc braced himself. "I'm sorry," he said, "but this is nothing more than extortion! I won't pay you a penny, gentlemen, nor this Señor Durán of yours." He turned away. "Good evening to you."

McVie laughed. "But it would be so easy for us to take it all, señor," Chacón said. He let the heel of his right hand rest on the butt of his Colt.

"Not so easy as you think!" It was Judy's voice, taut and snapping with anger like the tent cracking in the wind. The men turned.

From somewhere she had pulled Doc's twelve-gauge side-by-side shotgun. She was holding it waist level. the rabbit-ear hammers drawn full back. The three Thieves unconsciously sucked in their bellies. "You men clear out," she said.

"You talked us into it, señorita." Chacón grinned.

"You being most unreasonable, my frien'," Abadón said to Doc. "We will take what is ours. Why you not make it easy on yourself?"

Doc stayed silent. Abadón turned his head to Judy and licked his lips with a tongue like a small skinned animal. "And you, *querida*. You have much fire. I admire that very much." He nodded slowly. "We go. *Hasta la vista*." He turned deliberately and walked away. After a moment the others followed.

The night quickly swallowed them. Doc slumped against the hull of the wagon. "That was close." He shook his head. "What a fool I was, to get caught without my gun."

"You couldn't very well wear it on stage."

He smiled weakly. "Thanks for stepping in. You've got a steady hand with a shotgun."

She dropped her eyes. "Thanks."

He sighed, stretched. "Well, we'd better get cracking with the tent, before the wind carries it off to Arizona."

Judy stood a moment, then let in the hammers expertly with her thumb. "Those animals will be back."

"Count on it."

She laid the shotgun back inside the wagon and looked at the tent. "Shall we?"

Doc nodded and forced a smile. All he could think about was Abadón looking at Judy with those obsidian eyes of his. The giant had more than money on his mind.

And Doc honestly wondered whether he could be kept from collecting it.

CHAPTER SIX

It was past midnight before Doc and Judy got the tent broken down and everything stashed away. "You go on to bed," Doc told her, all chivalry even though his muscles were aching and his eyelids had turned to lead. "I'll take a final turn around camp and make sure everything's secure."

She gave him a weary smile. There was a smudge of grime across the bridge of her nose that made her look very young and vulnerable—and utterly desirable. He fought down the impulse to kiss her with all that his fatigue had left him of willpower. *She's not just a very proper young lady*, he told himself, *she's also your partner. You can't foul up your working relationship by making a pass at her.*

But, damn, she's beautiful.

A moment passed. She dropped her eyes. "Thank you." Her voice was slightly rough. Exhaustion, Doc guessed. He gave her a hand up into the wagon, picked up the shotgun, and started walking.

Judith was lying down a few yards from the wagon, sleeping. He walked up to her, knelt for a moment to croon to her and scratch behind her long ears. "Hey, sweetheart. You were a good girl tonight. I'm sorry I had to tie you up during the show, but you know how nervous loud noises make you. I didn't want you to get spooked and go running off, maybe break a leg in a prairie-dog hole."

She stirred and blew on his hand. Her huge liquid eyes

looked into his for a moment, as if forgiving him his lack of trust in her. Then she nuzzled him affectionately, put her nose down, and went back to sleep.

He walked down to the creek that ran behind the wagon, knelt for a moment to lay the shotgun down and splash water on his face. It was a clear, cool night. The year was too early yet for frogs to be out. The only sound was the musical murmur of the water, and the ever present western wind singing in the trees and sighing in the grass.

He shook his head and straightened, recovering the shotgun. Unbidden, the image of Judy Holiday's face sprang into his mind, accompanied by an all-too-familiar tightening in his loins. He grimaced.

That's one thing I can say for Rade without reservation, he told himself with a sardonic grin. *There's not the slightest danger of my falling in love with him.*

He began a circuit of the wagon, wondering how his partner was doing. *He's probably off at Señora Hortensia's this very minute, with Mandy Sue Farthington's painted lips wrapped around his dick. She sounds like the kind he goes for.* His own manhood gave a poignant throb. *Shit. I'd better stay off the subject of sex entirely, as long as I'm on this assignment with Judy—with Miss Holiday, that is.*

"Evenin'."

The shotgun was to his shoulder with the hammers full back before it dawned on him that he knew that low, slow voice. "Raider!" he hissed.

"Naw, it's the ghost of Maximilian the First, Emperor of Mexico," came the familiar drawl. "Got sick of the scenery down to Querétaro."

Doc's eyes, never too keen, had begun to pick the figure of Raider and his mount out of the darkness. "You stupid son of a bitch, I almost blew you in half!"

Raider swung off his bay. "You do that, they're gonna dock your pay, pardner," he said imperturbably.

"Whatever possessed you to come sneaking in here like that?"

Raider shrugged, as if to say, *It's jest my way.* And it

was. Though he hotly denied that so much as a drop of
Indian blood ran in his veins, he had many of the ways of
a Plains warrior, to go with his looks. Mounted or afoot,
he moved with the silence of a stalking puma. "What's
got up your butt, Doc?" he asked amiably, and dallied his
reins around the saddle horn. The bay put his head down
and began to crop.

Doc winced and looked around. No sign of Judy. "Watch
your language," he reproved.

"That's the worse Miss Holiday hears on this little
jaunt, we might as well pack it in and head back for St.
Lou. Mean we was tryin' to investigate the Las Peñas
Ladies' Auxiliary." He walked over to the wagon. "What
the hell's happent here? You're jumpy as a long-tailed cat
at a barn dance. And where's that little fluff?"

"I'm here," a voice said from the dark cave of the
wagon. "I'd be obliged if you'd speak of me with more
respect, Operative Raider. Otherwise I might not hold my
fire, the next time you creep up on the camp like a
Comanche."

There was a multiple cricket-click of metal on metal.
Raider paled a little under his trail tan. A moment later
Judy appeared at the tailgate, holding an octagonal-barrel
Winchester. "Evenin', ma'am," he said.

He gallantly held up a hand to help her down. She
ignored the offer, hiked up her skirt, and clambered down
as agilely as a monkey. "What do you want? Dr.
Weatherbee has had a long day."

Raider pursed his lips and gave Doc a fish eye. "Well,
you'll have to excuse me. I thought ol' Doc was an
operative fer the Pinkerton National Detective Agency,
and come here to consult about our assignment. Now, if
I'm makin' a mistake—"

"Cut the crap," Doc snapped. "We've already found
out a lot about this town. None of it very comforting."

Raider pulled down the tailgate and sat on it while Doc
and Judy took turns telling their story of the day's events.
The way Raider cocked an eyebrow at Judy's description

of Mandy Sue gave Doc a smug flash. He knew his partner clear down to the bootsoles.

Raider sobered up quickly when it came to the visit by Abadón and his companions after the medicine show. "I've heard about them *hombres*," he said. "McVie and Chacón are gunslingers, mankillers pure and simple. The Mex'd as soon kill you as look at you. The kid sooner." He rubbed the harsh stubble on his chin with a crackling sound. "And the big fu—uh—fella, Abadón. He's s'posed to be bad medicine. The worst."

"I can believe it," Judy said. "The way he looked at me—he's not human."

Doc felt a pang of concern for the lovely agent. "What have you learned, Rade?"

It was Raider's turn to tell of his experiences. He told of what he'd found out since coming to Las Peñas, about the Forty Thieves, about their interest in him, about Clarence King's approach and the trip to the Castile. His narrative was fairly straightforward and factual, though he had to play it up for Holiday some. Holiday watched and listened with cool reserve, her attitude one of professional detachment rather than disdain. Whatever she felt for her co-operative, she was paying full attention to the information he had to relay.

"Ol' Redeye, he turned up while I was drinkin' over to Ramona's this evenin'. He shoulda been called White-eye, tonight anyhow. You could see the whites of his eyes all the way around. He was plumb scared."

"What of?" Judy asked.

Raider shrugged. "Figger he'd been counted on to recruit me. I don't think this Durán feller takes too kindly to failure. He's got some of the hardest-looking *hombres* workin' for him that ever I laid eyes on, and they all walks around him like they's li'l gray mice and he's King Cat, in person. And that sister of his—hell—uh, hey, she's an eyeful enough to make a statue of Winfield Scott climb down off'n his horse, but the only thing anybody ever talks about her is how crazy she is. Don't know but what these here Thieves're more afraid of her than brother Henry.

"Anyhow, Clarence, he hunted me up. 'You gotta reconsider, Rade,'' he told me, practically slobberin' on my sleeve. 'You don't know these people. They don't stand fer no competition.' "

" 'Well,' says I, 'reckon we can come to some sort of agreement.'

" 'When the first spadeful of dirt lands on that Indian face of yours,' he says, 'that's when they'll come to terms with you, brother.' He went on to tell me stories about some of the men they got riding in Durán's string already. Ones like McVie, Chacón, Toby Sublette. Some of 'em we've heard of: Grant Largo, who's wanted for that Wells Fargo job in California; Preacher Hanks, killed all those people in the Dakotas two years ago during a mine-payroll heist; Vincente Dominguín, that *guerrillero* out of Chihuahua, likes to tie people over the spike of a *maguey* plant.''

"Why does he do that?" Holiday asked.

Raider showed his teeth in an expression that was not a smile. "The central shoot of a *maguey*—your century plant, ma'am—it's tough and woody and got a sort of a thorny hard cap on it. Grows up to ten, twelve feet a night." The female operative paled a little and swallowed hard when the implications of that sank in.

"The worst of all of them is Marcosio Abadón. Say he's seven feet of pure undiluted hell. Word is small animals hide when he walks abroad, birds fall out of the sky when he looks at them, and if he breathes on a sapling it just curls up and dies.''

"I can believe it," Doc said grimly. He took a cheroot from his breast pocket, scratched a match alight on one of the rusted cleats in the wagon hull, and lit up. Raider scowled at him briefly and moved upwind.

"Don't nobody know where he comes from. They say he's the son of a *brujo* witchman and La Llorona, the Weeping Lady—that's kind of a she-demon they got in these parts, ma'am, walks the night with a lantern wailin'

for her lost kids and tryin' to lure men to their doom.
When he was a baby he was found under a mesquite bush
with a strangled rattlesnake in his hand. That sort of
thing—you know the way men brag on bad men. But with
Abadón, it somehow don't seem so much like jest wind.''

''So what did you tell Mr. King?'' Holiday asked.

Raider laughed. ''Jest shrugged him off. 'Thanks fer the
tip, hombre. Can I buy you a drink?' Didn't seem minded
to drink with me, so I let him go.''

Holiday frowned. ''You're sure that was wise?''

''What was I supposed to do? Throw down on him?''

''No, no. But I thought you were going to try to infiltrate this outlaw band. Now you're turning them down
when they ask you to join.''

''Don't wanna make it too easy on them.'' He chuckled
at her surprised, almost outraged, expression. ''Naw, it
looks like I'm tryin' to worm my way in with their little
group, they'll be down on my neck *muy pronto*. This
Durán's as wary as a coyote bitch with a fresh litter, and
some o' the broncos he has runnin' with him are no
dummies neither. So I act like I don't wanna play their
game, like I'm set on goin' my own way. They're gonna
have to lean on me to get me into line.''

''Or kill you,'' she said.

He laughed again. ''They ain't yet. They was goin' to, I
never woulda got to ride out of the courtyard, up at the
Castile. And that li'l show I put on with that greaser knife
boy—Durán's gonna be droolin' to get me in his stable.''
He showed his teeth in a wolf's grin. ''I'd say sister
Sancha wouldn't mind having a new stud in the barn
neither. Leastaways, not the way she was lookin' at me.
She'da been pryin' my lips open for a gander at my teeth if
her brother hadn't turned up.''

Judy blushed and dropped her eyes. ''Beg your pardon,
ma'am. It's jest—well, I gets a little frisky, when I get a
whiff of danger. Don't mean to talk rough in front of
you.''

''That's quite all right,'' she said, a bit stiffly.

"Anyways—after I put up all that fuss about not wantin' in, who's gonna suspect it's what I'm been aimin' to do all along?"

Doc looked at Judy. A shallow frown still furrowed her brow. He couldn't decide whether she was surprised at such subtlety on the part of brash straightforward Raider, or whether she thought he was being *too* subtle. "Rade's been in this business a long time," he said. "He knows the ropes."

She bit her lip. "Excuse me for doubting." Doc couldn't tell if her tongue was in her cheek or not.

"Well," Raider said, stretching and stifling a yawn. "Gotta get back to Wideman's. Had a long day today."

We might all have a longer one tomorrow," Doc replied, yawning himself and hiding it behind his fist.

If either of them knew how prophetic his words were, none of them would have gotten much sleep that night.

"I'd like to see the chief of police," Doc announced. The sunken-chested shirt-sleeved man with the star on his vest kept writing in his logbook. Doc reached down with the tip of his walking stick and snapped the book shut.

"Hey!" the man looked up in outrage, going red to the tips of his protuberant ears. "You can't do that!"

"I said I would like to see the chief of police," he repeated.

"But, but—my book!"

"I wanted to be sure of securing your attention. I feared you were deaf." He reached inside his spiffy pin-striped blue coat and produced a card engraved with gilt letters. He handed it over. The skinny carrot-haired policeman squinted at it.

"It says, 'Dr. Weatherbee, Physician, Healer, Compounder of Balms and Specifics, Discoverer of the Patented Egyptian Cure.' I believe that's an adequate summary of my credentials. Now, who might *you* be, to try to obstruct an upstanding citizen in his attempt to speak with your chief?"

The policeman's receding lower jaw pumped fruitlessly, and his poached eyes glared indignation over the half-moons of his reading glasses. His outrage was so great that he couldn't find words; random gargles and squeaks were all that emerged from his carplike mouth.

"What's going on out there?" a bluff voice boomed from behind the policeman's narrow shoulders. "You havin' troubles, Charlie?"

The waiting room of the police station was cramped, with the clerk's spindle-shanked desk, a potbellied stove, a spittoon, and a few uncomfortable chairs crowded on its scuffed hardwood floor. A door led past the green-blottered desk. The doorway was abruptly filled by a tall figure in a gray sack coat, white shirt with black string tie, black vest, brown trousers, and boots. The newcomer was broad of shoulder and gut, with a clean-shaven face like a slab of beef and a shock of white hair on top.

"This clown was givin' me trouble, Chief!" Charlie yipped. He jumped to his feet and assumed a feet-wide, pugnacious stance. "I was just about to pitch him out on his ass."

The chief nodded indulgently. "Sure you were, Charlie, sure you were." He looked at Doc. His eyes were small, and watery blue, and a deal more intelligent than the rest of him.

"What's your beef, mister?" he asked, not unfriendly.

"I wish to register a complaint, sir. Your . . . subordinate . . . did not see fit to heed my requests to speak with you."

The chief looked at Charlie, standing there like a banty-cock, and then down at Charlie's desk. "Thought you was supposed to be bringin' the logs up to date, Charlie?" He nodded heavily at the closed black ledger.

Charlie's prominent Adam's apple dipped and swooped. "But, Chief, I—he—that is—"

"That's all right." The chief patted him on the shoulder with a bearlike paw. "Just don't let me catch you slackin' off again, okay?'' He looked at Doc. ''Come on back to my office, mister. We'll talk.''

He waved for Doc to precede him down a short corridor. It passed a door on the left that was slightly ajar, with W. EDWARD BROWARD, CHIEF OF POLICE inscribed on it in inch-high black-letter, and led to a heavy door, reinforced with iron. Through the barred grating Doc glimpsed a further corridor with cells on either side. He couldn't tell if any were occupied or not.

Broward stopped and pushed the partly open door wide. ''Come on in and set a spell.''

''Thank you, Chief.'' Doc stepped into the office, removing his black derby as he did so. It was a small office, more claustrophobic than the front room, featuring a mound of papers, fliers, wanted posters, and the like, under which Doc presumed a desk was somewhere to be found; a chair behind the mound for Broward with gunbelt slung over the back and a filing cabinet next to it, convenient to the occupant's right hand; another chair on this side for visitors; all squeezed between walls Doc didn't think widely enough spaced to accommodate the chief's shoulders.

Broward sidled past him and seated himself behind the desk. When Doc remained standing he waved a big hand in the chair. ''Go on, sit, sit.'' He pulled open the bottom drawer of the filing cabinet and rummaged around inside. Above the cabinet was a rifle rack that held two Winchester 73s—a carbine and a rifle—and a long-barreled side-by-side shotgun. Above the chief's chair was a framed photograph of the white-haired Broward standing in front of a large desk, shaking hands with a stern-visaged man Doc recognized as General Lew Wallace, the territory's outgoing auctorial governor.

Straightening, Broward noted the direction of Doc's gaze. He grinned. It was a boyish grin, disarming, the kind that took you right into the man's confidence. ''Guess I got to get me a new one o' those,'' he said. ''Soon as Garfield's man comes out to pick up the reins.'' He scooted papers to the side to make a bare space and set down a whiskey bottle and two shot glasses. He poured one glass full, poised the bottle above the other one, and lifted a bushy eyebrow in inquiry.

"It's rather early in the day," Doc murmured. The Chief shrugged and started to set the bottle down. "On the other hand, I refuse to play the slave to custom."

Grinning his infectious grin, the chief poured the second glass perilously full and handed it across to Doc without spilling a single amber drop on the piled papers. Doc accepted it with an appraising look in his eye. Chief Broward had the florid face and broken-veined nose of a man who went a lot of rounds with drink and generally lost, but his hands were steady as a rock. *Something to remember*, Doc thought. He sipped.

Broward emptied his glass with a practiced wrist-flick, shuddered, sighed, and wiped his mouth with the back of his hand. "What can I do for you, sir?" he asked.

Doc produced another ivory-colored card. "I am Dr. Weatherbee," he began.

Broward raised his hand and waved away both card and explanation. "I know who you are," he said. "You're the medicine man got his wagon parked over to the Widow Whateley's lot. That's a mighty strange old gal, son; rumor says she got her a weird young'un, she keeps locked up all the time, never lets out, never lets no one see. But you know how these mountains are; all full of wild talk and scary-stories. It's them Mexicans. Superstitious bunch."

He poured himself another shot. "You got that green-eyed Gypsy titty-girl, too. Heard me a thing or two about that dance she put on last night, with the cobra." He socked the booze back and laughed. "Guess I might wander out one o' these nights and catch your show. Ain't had so much excitement in these parts in many moons."

He shook his head. "Don't know what it is. First poor old Hugo blows hisself and his tavern halfway to Albuquerque. Then you turn up with your medicine show . . ."

His brow crumpled thoughtfully and his voice trailed off. *Whoops!* Doc thought. *I can't even let him begin to suspect more than a coincidental connection.* "That's what I came to speak to you about," he said quickly. "My medicine show, as you termed it."

"What's the problem."

"Last night after my lecture and Madame Teresa's dance, a trio of ruffians approached me and demanded that I pay them protection money." He let a ringing note of indignation— altogether genuine, at that—creep into his voice. "They threatened me!"

Broward frowned. "These yahoos—what'd they look like?" His puffy eyelids half covered his small watery eyes.

Doc described them. The police chief's gaze grew more and more hooded. "I know them," he said slowly, when Doc was finished. "They work for Mr. Durán, owns a ranch a few miles out of town. Cowhands."

If even one of those men has spent an hour of his life herding cattle that he hadn't just cut out of somebody else's herd, I'm John the Baptist. "They looked like common ruffians to me."

Broward shrugged. "Reckon they were just funnin' you. Chaffin' the stranger in town." He shrugged ponderously. "You know how these small towns out in the sticks are. Hasslin' newcomers's 'bout all the excitement there is."

"But they *threatened* me."

Broward frowned. "Now, you think hard, mister." The bluff friendliness had vanished from his voice. "You're makin' a serious charge here. What precisely did these fellas threaten you *with?*"

Doc opened his mouth—and stopped dead. *They didn't threaten me with anything*, he remembered suddenly. *I think they were about to get down to specifics when Judy showed up with the double-gun.* "Why, they didn't threaten me with anything in particular," Doc sputtered. "They— they acted in a menacing way, and gave me very definitely to understand that it would go hard with me if I failed to pay them."

Broward was leaning back in his chair, drumming heavy

fingers on his desktop. "Now, you're new in town," he said, "and I got to admit you're performin' a valuable public service, livenin' up the lives of the honest people of Las Peñas. So I'll go easy on you." He leaned forward, sinking his elbows into the mire of documents.

"I won't run you in for traipsin' in here makin' unfounded charges against solid citizens of the territory," he rumbled, "this time. Understand?"

Doc rested both hands on the knob of his cane. "Fully."

Again the grin flashed. "Knew I could count on you, Doc," he said. He pushed back the chair and grunted to his feet. "Ah, my achin' back. I ain't as young as I used to be, mister." He massaged the small of his back with one big hand. "Ain't nowhere near so young."

His eyes met Doc's, and the Pink read supplication in them. He glanced away, to a second photograph on the wall opposite the gun rack. It showed three dead men, obvious desperadoes with sweeping mustaches and rifles across their chests, lying on the boardwalk of a nameless store. Beside them stood a much younger Ed Broward, grinning with that same grin, with a Henry rifle grounded by one boot like a hunter standing over his kill. Next to the photo was framed a newspaper clipping, yellowing with age. The headline read, "TOWN MARSHAL BREAKS GANG: Hurley Boys Meet Timely End in Pitched Gun-Battle."

Doc stood up. "I understand."

"I knew I could count on you." Broward stuck out his hand. "See you one of these nights, Doctor."

Doc's urge was to refuse to take the proferred hand, but somehow he couldn't bring himself not to. He shook it briefly. Broward's grip was cold and clammy. "Good afternoon, Chief."

Waving a huge hand, Broward stuffed his bulk back into the chair. He was pouring himself another drink as Doc left.

Hungry after his encounter with the law in Las Peñas, Doc wandered into the Silver King for a meal and a lager beer. It was early in the day for lunch. There were one or two loafers propped on the bar, and a half-hearted poker game going on in the corner. There were also two armed men sitting in another corner, laughing and talking louder than the rest of the barflies combined, a stocky sandy-mustached Anglo and a brown-skinned man, Mexican or *nativo*, who though about Doc's height possessed enormous shoulders, bigger than Abadón's, perhaps, and a neck so thick that his head appeared to come to a point on top. He had a robust black mustache and a curl of lank black hair that lay in the middle of his forehead.

Doc carefully ignored them as he ate his *huevos rancheros*, and they seemed to pay no attention to him. As he was halfway through his eggs and second beer, served by a simpering teenaged girl with a lumpy-looking body and dirty blond hair, two more obvious Thieves entered. Both were on the short side, with dark skin and Indian-straight jet-black hair. Both had on loose cotton shirts and pants that looked like pajamas, and sombreros slung across their backs. One wore sandals, the other boots. Both had gunbelts cinched around their narrow waists, with wicked-looking knives stuck through them. *Mexicans*, Doc judged, as opposed to *nativos*, who were born in the States. Probably a couple of *campesinos* from one of the northern states, Chihuahua or Sonora, desert-toughened peasants, resourceful and independent-minded, disinclined to push a fight against bad odds—from common sense, not cowardice— but capable of the craziest kind of back-to-the-wall bravery. They gave Doc a quick glance and went over to sit with their two companions.

The new arrivals were getting rowdy as Doc rose to leave. The sandaled Mexican had his arm around the waitress's waist, and was burbling endearments to her in misshapen English, while his comrade and the Anglo laughed. The burly *nativo* scowled with his chin on his massive chest. There was little love lost between the native Spanish and their cousins from across the border.

"Miss," he said, not loudly, but projecting strongly. "My reckoning please."

The girl tore herself away. The Mexican made as if to hurl himself after her. His friend put a restraining hand on his arm. He resisted for a moment, then sat down again, laughing, as the waitress came up to Doc, brushing tears from her eyes.

"That'll be fifty cents, sir." She tried to smile. Her eyes were chocolate-brown, and very pretty.

He handed her a silver dollar. "Thank you," he said, and walked out before she could offer change.

He stood a moment blinking into the late-morning sunlight. The streets were fairly empty. People didn't have to hide from the noonday heat yet, but midday was always inclined to be a lazy time. He straightened his tie, settled his hat at an appropriate angle on his head, and set off at a brisk walk.

He had turned left off Central, the town's main street, onto Pecos, a north-south side street that would put him on the edge of town nearest Widow Whateley's field and his wagon, when three men stepped out of an alley in front of him. His heart sank. All three wore pistol belts.

They fanned out to block his passage. "Please excuse me," Doc said briskly.

"In a hurry, mister?" the one in the middle asked. He was a skinny man an inch or two taller than Doc—a breed, by the look of him—with a drooping mustache and a drooping left eyelid.

The man on his right said something in Spanish, too fast and slurred for Doc to catch. He was Doc's height, and lean, dressed like a typical *norteño* gunfighter; tight black pants decorated with bright silver buttons running down the legs, a red sash with his gunbelt worn over it, white shirt and embroidered black vest, red scarf at throat, sweeping sombrero. The half-breed laughed, showing stained snaggled teeth. "Pablo here says you shouldn't be so rude. Or does our company offend you?"

He laughed again—and suddenly his right fist was flashing toward Doc's face.

Doc sidestepped, blocked the punch with his walking stick, and then slammed the silver knob into the side of the half-breed's head. The man crossed his eyes and went down as if poleaxed.

The other two, the Mexican on Doc's left and the chunky *nativo* on his right, closed in. Doc feinted for the garishly clad Mexican, then suddenly swung his cane with one hand near the tip. It whipped down and up, straight between the *nativo*'s jeans-clad legs. The man's eyes bulged. *"Hijo de la Madre,"* he gasped, and his knees buckled.

Snarling a curse, the Mexican lunged forward. Doc fended him off with the cane and danced away. The man he'd got in the crotch made a grab for him. Doc gave him credit for fortitude and a vicious stroke across the face. The man fell over, moaning.

Doc and the Mexican circled one another. The Mexican was spitting like an angry cat. Doc wondered whether he ought to go for the pistol with the cut-down barrel he wore in his left armpit. *Better not*, he told himself. *Chief Broward would probably chuck my butt in the jug for putting a hole through one of Durán's mortal saints*. He'd keep an eye out lest the other went for a knife or the pistol at his own side, though—better arrested than perforated.

The Mexican made a few half-hearted feints for Doc's face. He would have preferred to fight with gun or knife, Doc knew, like any sane man. *Looks as if Durán wants me alive*.

Strong arms wrapped around his chest, pinioning his arms to his side. "Okay boys!" a voice cried in his ear. "I got him fer ya!"

Head swimming from the reek of whiskey, Doc waited as the Mexican bravo, smiling hugely, closed in. He kicked him in the balls, then smashed his foot down on the instep of the man who was holding him. The grip loosened. He brought the cane knob sharply up under the man's chin.

Teeth cracked together and he was free. He gave the man at his back the point of the cane in his belly, and turned.

A cannonball struck him in the face. He staggered back. The big-shouldered *nativo* from the bar stood in front of him, a mild, puzzled frown wrinkling his forehead beneath his forelock. The sandy-haired Anglo who had been drinking with him lay in the dust, clutching his gut and gagging.

The two *campesinos* who had come into the Silver King as Doc lunched ran at him like wolves going for a stricken elk. He jabbed one in the throat with his cane tip. The man clutched at his neck and fell, face going purple. The other shouted an obscenity and whipped out a knife.

The burly man hit him behind the ear. "*Jodido!*" he roared as the man sprawled at his feet. He stepped over him and advanced on Doc, arms outspread.

His stomach churning, head ringing like a carillon, Doc thwacked the man on the point of his head, knocking his hat off. A trickle of blood ran down between black eyes.

The man smiled.

Frantically, Doc hacked at him again. The big man brought a burly forearm up. The fine hardwood of the cane snapped across it. The man smiled even more broadly, then stepped forward.

Dimly Doc saw a fist coming for his face. It moved with a peculiar slowness, as though through molasses. He tried to raise his arms to ward it off, but they were numb, were lead, too slow.

The fist became a moon, filling Doc's vision. Light exploded behind his eyes. A black pit yawned before him. He fell into it.

And fell, and fell.

CHAPTER SEVEN

"Buy a girl a drink?" Raider looked up sharply from the table where he was locked in solitary combat with a bottle of bourbon. Suspicion glittered in his dark eyes.

It died at once when he caught sight of the tall, red-headed woman who stood next to his table. The proprietor of Las Peñas's second-best saloon was not exactly Raider's vision of the ideal woman—big, blond, and bosomy—but in ways she was a little closer than sparrowlike little Hannah Parker. She was tall and slender-built, generous about the hips, with breasts like large ripe fruits swinging freely beneath the none-too-high-cut bodice of her plain blue cotton dress. She had an oval face, lordly straight nose, high cheekbones, and slanted almond eyes as dark as Raider's. Her hair was copper-colored, darker than Judy Holiday's, with that odd brassy tint that marked the bearer as having *tlaxcalteca* Indian blood in her veins.

Her name was Ramona Tixier. Her surname was *nativo* of a few years' standing. The family had been founded by a French-Canadian *coureur de bois* who had wandered down from what was now Colorado back in the early part of the century. The Frenchman was quickly assimilated, and his line had become prosperous and well respected. Somewhere along the way Ramona's branch had picked up its copper hair from descendants of Mexican Indians of the defunct city-state of Tlaxcala, who, after helping Cortéz destroy the Aztec empire, had come north in later centuries as mercenaries employed against the Apache and Comanche.

Ramona was forty-five years old and had buried three husbands. The years—and marriages—had left few marks on her. There were tiny crow's-feet around her eyes, and her skin was no longer as creamy-soft as when she had been a wild girl, driving all the *vaqueros* crazy at fandangos—and a select few even crazier, out on a bed of fallen pine needles beneath the stars and moon, coupling like a she-panther. She was a little mellower, too, not as tempestous or volcanic-tempered as that girl had been. She was just about as beautiful a woman as Raider had ever seen, brown, white, red, or striped.

She seemed to think Raider was just about her size, too.

"Sit down." His chair scraped back and he stood up. The other few drinkers huddled around their afternoon whiskeys glanced up with varying degrees of jealousy. Ramona's favors were eagerly sought, but rarely given. Even the Forty Thieves treated her with a certain respect— whether because she was a cousin of Henry Durán, or because there was no doubt that anybody who tried to force himself on her had better kiss his *cojones* good-bye. He might kill her—but he could never take her against her will.

She smiled and plunked a bottle of tequila, a glass, and a small ceramic bowl of salt down on the red-checked tablecloth. "Have a real drink, and give that gringo swill a rest."

He sat down again. "Shore." She produced a big butcher knife and cut a lime in half. He took half, polished off his whiskey, and let her pour the yellowish liquor into his glass.

Raider watched her. He liked the way she looked, the way she moved. They had been circling around each other since he'd turned up, each instinctively liking the other, each strongly attracted, but wary by nature. He knew and she knew that they'd end up in bed, and before too much time had passed. It gave him a comfortable feeling to look at her.

She raised her glass. He took a bite of the salt he'd poured on the web of his left hand, took a shot of the tequila, then sucked at the lime. She did the same, her eyes locked on his. The way she worked at the lime with her full red lips made his crotch go taut. The way her eyes danced showed she knew it.

Eyes. He had this gorgeous redheaded Mexican piece in front of him, just waiting for him to say the word to her to yell to her assistant Jorge to take over and drag him into her little room in the back with its *santos* and its painting of the Virgin of Guadalupe, and fuck him till he couldn't stand. And all he could think of were Sancha Durán's eyes—yellow, and crazy, promising infinite delight and infinite torment.

Shit, he thought, as Ramona poured another drink. *Been hangin' around with Doc too long. I'm startin' to go on like one of them philosophical fellers.*

"Have you found work yet?" Ramona asked. She caressed him with her eyes. He had first wandered into Ramona's two days after arriving in town. It was a compact adobe block of a building just north of the main drag and a little west of the plaza. Not as pretentious as the Silver King, which catered to the Town Hall crowd, such as it was; nonetheless, Ramona's was more to Raider's liking. It was a neat, cheery, comfortable little place. It had low smoke-stained *vigas*, spotless whitewashed walls, little tables with red and white checked oilcloth spreads on them, wildflowers in small earthenware vases on most of them. It had a small bar—local pine, nothing fancy—with an assortment of bottles on shelves in the back, with sullen Jorge Ramírez and a plump, pretty Pueblo Indian girl named Roberta to help out.

Mostly, it had Ramona.

Raider shrugged and picked up the refilled glass. "Had an offer yesterday."

"From whom?"

"Durán."

For a second it looked as if she might drop her glass. She paled. Spots of red showed at the points of her aristocratic cheekbones. "What did you tell him?" she asked. Her eyes were narrowed to burning slits.

Raider lapped up salt, drank, squeezed the lime into his mouth. "Told him no."

She relaxed. "I'm glad. I know you're a stranger, Raider, that I know nothing about you. Still . . . I feel that I know you, a little. And I would not like to think you are of the sort who would choose to ride with Henry Durán and his Forty Thieves."

"Mostly I prefer to go my own way."

She smiled and reached a hand to pat his wrist. "I think that's why I like you so," she purred. "I—"

A man's hand caught her by the wrist and pulled her hand away from Raider's. "What d'you think you're doin', you cheap Meskin slut?" a drink-slurred voice demanded. "Whorin' around after this damned outsider?"

Ramona's eyes blazed with anger. "Take your hand off me, Dick Rynerson!"

"I think you better do like the lady says, mister," Raider said, his voice deadly low. He was staring through narrowed eyes at a tall, lanky gringo with gray-shot mouse-colored hair sticking anywhichway out from under his hat. He had squint eyes, prominent ears, and a salt and pepper mustache sprouting from beneath a large fleshy nose. The smell of cheap whiskey hung around him like a cloud, as if he'd bathed in the stuff. *Likely he has*, Raider thought. *I'm bein' set up—he ain't no drunker than I am*.

Because the interloper had a Colt Peacemaker hanging from his right hip. Durán had decided what to do about the holdout. Apparently Raider had just lost his bet as to what the top Thief's decision would be.

The man Ramona called Dick Rynerson smiled thinly. "Well, I guess I better do like the high-and-mighty gennulman says," he sneered. He let go of the woman's wrist. She pulled it away and began rubbing it, as if to wipe germs from it. "You're awful tony, mister. Maybe you'll be good enough to drink with me?" He picked up the open tequila bottle and tossed it at Raider's face.

Raider caught it one-handed. "You get out of here, Rynerson," Ramona said in a voice of pure poison. Rynerson backhanded her across the face, left-handed.

His right whipped out his gun, quick as a striking snake.

No sooner had Raider caught the bottle than he realized how neatly he'd been mousetrapped. He dropped it as if it were red-hot, but already it was too late. The other man's six-gun was clearing leather before the bottle was out of his hand.

Lashing out with desperate strength Raider kicked the table with his right leg. It flew up and caught Rynerson full in the chest, spilling the salt bowl and glasses and whiskey bottle to shatter on the floor.

Rynerson's gun blasted. Raider heard the shot moan wide, but even as it crashed out he was yanking out his own piece, hauling back the trigger, and working the hammer with his thumb.

Four shots cracked out almost as one. Four splintery holes appeared in the bottom of the table, before it fell away with a crash. Dick Rynerson flew back against the stuccoed adobe wall as if he'd been struck by a train.

For a moment he hung there like a marionette from its strings. A black hole showed in the slight bulge of his belly just above the hand-tooled black leather of his gunbelt, in the middle of a scarlet stain spreading into the white and brown and gray plaid flannel of his shirt. A similar hole leaked red right around the skinny man's wishbone. A third hole, blue-black, weeped a thin stream of red across his left eyebrow and down into his staring blue eye. His stomach crawling, Raider watched the red stream crawl right across the eyeball. Dick Rynerson didn't so much as blink. There was no Dick Rynerson there *to* blink.

There was a scream, feminine and shrill, as the body toppled to the floor, carrying another table with it with a crash.

Raider was at Ramona's side in a single pantherish bound. She was still picking herself up, her hair practically standing on end in her fury. "That pig. That *pinche*! I hope you killed him! I—"

She broke off as her eyes found the blood spatters on the walls against which Rynerson had spent his last few second upright. "Oh," she said, in a faltering voice. Then: "It served him right."

Raider put his arm around her shoulder. She flowed against him. He felt the stirring in his loins that he so often felt after combat. The warm smell of her was heavy and sweet in his nostrils, and he thought he caught the musky whiff of excitement. Maybe she was reacting the same way he was. Maybe he should take her on back to the little room with its portrait of the Virgin and—

"What's going on here?"

Raider and Ramona both looked to the door. Two men stood there. Both wore gunbelts, but these two had six-pointed silver stars on their vests. One, a lanky, square-faced man in black suit and bowler, with a mustache that completely hid his mouth, had a sawed-off double-barreled shotgun tucked under his arm.

Roberta stopped screaming and fled back into the kitchen. "My God," said the second cop. He was a short wiry man with a belly that stuck out, not because it was fat, but because its owner stood and walked with an odd curve in his back. He strutted over to the cooling body and knelt beside it. He turned it over on its back. "My God!" he exclaimed. "It's Dick Rynerson. He's been murdered!"

"*Murdered*?" Ramona's voice rang with outrage. "He was defending himself!"

Suddenly the double-gun was in the mustached policeman's hand. "Better drop it, mister!" He gestured with the twin muzzles at the still-smoking revolver clutched in Raider's left hand.

Raider let the pistol fall. The cop with the bowed belly looked up from beside Dick Rynerson. "You're comin' with us," he said harshly. "I'm arrestin' you for the murder of Richard Rynerson!"

It was only then that Raider fully appreciated just how he'd been set up. He was actually grinning under his mustache as he meekly held out his hands for the little cop to slap the handcuffs on.

He almost had to admire the whole scheme. It was that neat.

He winked and nodded to Ramona, who was standing by cursing the police as they hustled Raider off. Then they pushed him out into the street and started him on the four-block march to the city jail.

Slowly Doc became aware of himself again. It was a mistake. His body felt like one solid bruise, and his head was crashing like the pistons of a locomotive.

"Ooh," he moaned, He wondered if he dared opened his eyes. He could see light filtering red through the lids. If he exposed his eyes to it, he had no doubt that his head would simply explode like an overpressure boiler.

"Is he awake? Is he awake, my child?" The voice was male, elderly, and nervous, tinged with an accent that Doc's still-scrambled wits could not place. That irritated him. He accounted himself an expert on accents. Before he could reconsider he forced his eyes open.

"Holy shit!" The words burst from his mouth as the light of a kerosene lamp stabbed through his eyes into his raw brain.

"Yes, father, I believe he is awake." This voice was young and feminine and pleasant, and not without a certain sarcasm.

He felt cool wetness bathe his eyes, his forehead. "Shade the poor man's face, for God's sake."

The soothing damp was withdrawn. There was the sound of the lantern's hanger disengaging from a wall hook, and the weight of the yellow glare came off his eyelids. He sighed with relief and opened his eyes.

His vision swam in a whirlpool blur. He frowned, tried

to make his eyes focus. Gradually the swirl within them resolved into a face. It was a woman's face—young, full-lipped, long, and finely sculpted, with an arrogant thrust of nose that on another might have appeared jarring. Instead it lent the face a marked exotic beauty that was complemented by large dark-brown eyes, slanted and long-lashed. The hair was hidden in a scarf tied round her head, but the woman's eyebrows were emphatic black arches.

"You're frowning," she said, showing pearly teeth. The ends of her full lips twitched. "I hope you like what you see more than *that*."

"Deborah!" The old man's voice was scandalized. "Oy! Do not be so immodest. We don't even know if—if—"

"We may safely assume he's a Gentile, Papa," she said, smiling openly. "Jews are few and far between in this part of the world."

Doc's vision was finally coming under control, and he definitely did like what he saw, especially since he was taking in more of the picture— the white cotton man's shirt with the sleeves rolled up, and jutting most alluringly over his face. *I wonder if she's checked to make* sure *I'm a Gentile*, he thought feverishly. *I'd sure be glad to prove it.*

He heard a fussy footfall and steeled himself to move his eyeballs to the right. It felt as if they were rolling in broken glass. A small gray man in a long black frock coat was standing next to the young woman at the side of the bed on which Doc lay. He stared down at Doc, fingering his long gray beard with long liver-spotted fingers.

Doc had placed the oldster's accent, with a little help from the lovely sloe-eyed Deborah. Eastern European Jewish— Ashkenazi. To Doc he did not look Jewish, unlike his daughter Deborah. He had a long, lined face, a straight thin nose above straight thin lips that were now twisted with apprehension and concern, fierce eyebrows, startlingly black, above his worried gray eyes. His hair was thin, topped with a little black knitted yarmulke at the crown of his long skull. He peered down at Doc through bifocals with square rims of gold wire.

"I—I'm very grateful to both of you," Doc said. It took great effort to speak. Each word rang like a hammer blow in his skull, and his tongue felt like a roll of socks someone had tried to stuff his mouth with.

The old man's eyes darted to the woman's face, then back to Doc. "It is nothing," he said. "But you must promise me this."

"What's that?"

"You must leave town at once."

Doc shook his head. Another mistake—his brains sloshed from one side of his head to the other, as if they'd been jarred loose from their moorings. He moaned and melted into the yielding embrace of the bed.

Deborah dipped a cloth into a bowl on the stand beside the bed and laved Doc's face with it. "Oh, Father," she chided. "You've upset him."

"Better upset than dead, for him. Look—see for yourself what those scoundrels did!"

"Haven't I been wiping the dirt and dried blood off him for the last half-hour?" she flared. Immediately she looked back to Doc and her face softened. "I'm sorry. I'll try to keep my voice down."

"I'm much obliged," Doc said weakly. "But I think I'd better be on my way. I don't wish to bring you folks any trouble." He tried to rise. Deborah put a firm but gentle hand in the middle of his chest and pushed him back down.

"Don't be *meshuga*, my boy," the old man said sternly. "You will not leave my house until you can walk with a chance of not falling on your face."

Doc essayed a weak smile. His mouth felt like a broken plate. He didn't want to think about how many of his teeth might have survived the beating the Thieves had given him. He remembered the burly *nativo*'s fist eclipsing the sun, and shuddered. From the state of his ribs and face, the blow that put his lights out had only been the beginning of a general fandango, featuring him as the dance floor.

"I'm Doc Weatherbee," he said. "To whom do I owe my undying gratitude?"

Deborah smiled, a bit wryly, but not unappreciatively. "I am Benjamin Silver," the old man said. "A merchant of many years' residence in Las Peñas. This is my daughter Deborah. She has no shame, but no girl has in these days. She is dutiful, in her own stubborn way."

Deborah looked at her father with a smile and shook her head. "I think I should try to sit up now," Doc said. "I don't want to become a permanent fixture in your home."

Deborah knelt beside him. Her breath was warm and sweet on his bruised cheek, and he felt one breast soft against his biceps. He liked the feeling. *Glad to know the old Adam's still capable of stirring*, he told himself. *Thought Durán's boys might've tried to put a cramp in his style*.

"Are you sure you feel like it?" she asked. "Papa is a nervous old woman, but if you wish I'll chase him out and we'll let you sleep a while longer."

"What time is it?" he asked.

Silver pulled out an immense silver turnip watch and peered at it. "Five minutes after four."

"Jesus." He sat up. Dizziness washed over his head. He reeled. Deborah's hand steadied him, strong and firm.

"You shouldn't be exerting yourself," she said.

"Ha—have to," he said, squeezing his eyes tightly shut. He felt if he squeezed them tightly enough some of the pain would be wrung out through his ears. "Got to get back to my wagon. Gotta do my show tonight."

Deborah frowned. "Show?"

Her father struck himself in the forehead with the heel of his hand. "Of course! What an old fool I am. You're the charla—the man with the traveling medicine show who came to town yesterday. I heard about the commotion you caused, with your colorful wagon and that Gypsy girl."

Deborah tensed and drew away slightly. "Gypsy girl?"

"My assistant," Doc said quickly. He moaned. "Friend of an old associate—God, water! My tongue's swollen like a balloon." Quickly Deborah poured a glass of water from a pitcher on the nightstand and held it to his lips. He watched her eyes as he sipped. She seemed to have accepted his explanation as to the presence of Judy Holiday in his wagon. Good. He was in rotten shape, but not *that* rotten.

His stomach was coming back to order. He had just about decided his head would never stop hurting, so he might as well try to function anyway. "I'm very grateful, but how did I happen to come here?" he asked.

Benjamin Silver looked away. "I—I watched those men beat you. I am an old man; there's nothing I could do." His own tone of voice called him a liar.

Doc shook his head, despite what it cost him. "Don't reproach yourself, Mr. Sivler. Those were Henry Durán's men, I'm sure of it. If you'd tried to help me you'd be a marked man. You did the only thing you could."

"Still." The old man shook his head. "Still, if it had not been for my daughter, perhaps . . . but that would have been wrong. Violence solves nothing. It only reduces one to the level of the animal. If only my son—" He stopped himself abruptly. "You gave a good account of yourself before they brought you down, my boy."

"Thanks." He was feeling himself all over now, trying to ascertain if anything was fractured or seriously out of place. "Wish I'd done just a bit better."

Silver frowned. "There were other people watching, as I was. They just stood there and let this thing happen."

Deborah patted his hand. "You know how it is, Father," she said. "You must not blame them. Or yourself."

He shook her off. "What I do not understand," he said, "is why you did not use *that*." Distaste was evident in his voice as he nodded to the open door of the bedroom. Doc's shoulder rig hung from the knob, with the double-action Colt still weighing down the holster.

Doc blinked in surprise. "What I want to know is why they didn't take it." He felt down his belly. The reassuring hardness of his watch was still in his vest pocket.

"I am sorry we couldn't change your clothes," Deborah said. "We had none that would fit you."

"They took nothing from you," Silver said. "Not even your wallet. They beat and kicked you for some minutes after you fell, until I feared they would kill you. Then they left."

So they were just trying to teach him a lesson. Among other things, they were trying to teach him that he wasn't worth disarming, or even rolling for walking-around money. He wasn't scared in the hoped-for manner. But he was impressed. There was a certain subtlety, a certain sophistication in what had been done to him.

Judy. Oh, God, what would they try to do to her?

"You simply cannot go yet, Dr. Weatherbee," Deborah said, clearly reading his intention in his eyes. Was it simply concern for his health that made her want him to stay? He hoped not.

For the first time he looked down at himself. He uttered a bitter curse. "Forgive me," he said at once. "But—look what they did to my shirt. And my *vest*. My God, what must my coat look like?"

"Terrible," said Deborah. She didn't try to hide her grin.

Old Mr. Silver reached out and took Doc's shoulder. "Better they should ruin your clothes than cause you permanent harm, my son."

Easy for you to say that, Doc thought indignantly. But he did not miss the way Deborah tensed when the old man called him *son*.

"You seem to know who was behind the attack," Deborah said.

"I haven't been in your fair city long," Doc replied, "but it didn't take long for me to become acquainted with your Forty Thieves."

Silver sucked in a breath. "Then you know of the curse which lies on our town." He squeezed Doc's shoulder tighter. "You know why you must leave."

"Now, wait a minute."

The old man shook his head doggedly. "You are already, as you say, a marked man. And what you said of Teresa, the girl—if that *golem* Abadón has cast envious eyes on her, the only hope for her is to fly." He looked at Deborah and quickly looked away. "I do not permit Deborah to walk the streets alone, or even at all if it can be helped. But I fear for her, especially since . . ." His words trailed off to nothingness again. "But there is no place for her to go, and she refuses to leave my side, disobedient vixen that she is."

"Oh, Father." Deborah shook her head and patted his hand. "Vixen indeed!"

"But you must go, Doctor."

Doc gathered his strength for a stab at standing. "I'm much obliged to you," he said guardedly. "But I hope you'll understand if I say I must make up my own mind whether to stay or go. I'm not minded to be hounded out of town by these ruffians."

The old man shook his head violently. "Pride! Is it worth dying for, then?" He grasped Doc's hand in both of his. "You can pay me back and at the same time save yourself and the girl."

"How can I do that?"

"You can take a message to Santa Fe. For me. And for the others."

"Oh, Papa!" Deborah cried in genuine alarm.

"Do you not trust this man? You did before I. I felt your heart soften even as Pancho and young Randolph brought him into our home, after I shamed them into helping me with him."

Deborah looked away. "What others?" Doc asked. For some reason his pulse had begun to race.

"Father . . ."

He waved her angrily away. "I will say it!" he insisted. "For those who were murdered! Their blood cries out for justice, and I cannot remain deaf."

"Who—who are you talking about?" Doc asked.

"The poor people who died at Hugo Ballenkamp's roadhouse. James and Warren and Odelbert and the Reverend Fitzhugh, and poor Hugo and María and Manuel." Tears shone in the old man's eyes. "For the ones Henry Durán had murdered."

CHAPTER EIGHT

Still limping, Doc made his way hurriedly from the Silver house through lengthening shadows toward the edge of town. He passed the spot where the Thieves had set on him earlier that day. Careless boots had scuffed out the blood spots, but the two halves of his walking stick were still lying there where he'd dropped them. He stopped, picked them up, stuck them under his arm, and walked on as briskly as his bruised legs could carry him.

He met a few people going about their end-of-day business. He was afraid of having to answer questions, or even being hauled off to jail. But no one seemed to want anything to do with him. Those he passed would barely so much as look at him. Life under the Forty Thieves seemed to have atrophied folks' sense of curiosity. Or perhaps the word had gone out that he had been punished, and to keep clear of him. He hoped not. He still had a medicine show to run, expenses to recoup.

Judy! Worry for her drove him onward when what he really wanted to do was find a nice door stoop and curl up on it and die. Or maybe go back to the Silver house and curl up with Deborah. He had the distinct impression she wouldn't have minded that, battered though he was. But he had to get back to his fellow operative.

When he reached the edge of town all he could see in Widow Whateley's field several hundred yards away was

the wagon and Judith, standing nearby cropping the grass.
There was no sign of Judy.

*If something had happened, surely Judith wouldn't be
acting so calm,* he told himself with out conviction. Fear
welled up inside him, black and ugly, goading him into a
run. He puffed down the slight incline from town, out of
breath almost at once in the thin mountain air, moving as
fast as his legs would carry him. It felt as if he was jolting
his body to pieces, but he would not let up on himself.

"Teresa," he called out as he neared the wagon.
"Teresa!" It took all his willpower not to call out *Judy*
instead, but he had to maintain her cover.

He stumbled, turned an ankle, kept running. Judith
raised her head and gazed at him. There was mild reproach
in her eyes for not greeting her first. Then again, she could
read the concern in his voice, so she decided to forgive
him his rudeness and went back to cropping the grama
grass.

He was almost at the wagon when Judy stepped down
from the front, the Winchester in her hand. "Doc," she
called with a wave. Then: "My God, what's *happened?*"

"Nothing," he lied. "Has anything happened here?"

She hesitated. "Three of our friends came by to visit
this afternoon. Chacón and a couple I hadn't seen before.
They asked if I wanted to go riding with them. I said no.
They said I'd better, or maybe I'd wind up with someone I
liked a lot less." Doc shuddered. "I showed them the
rifle, and they went away."

Doc reeled to the wagon, let down the tailgate, and sat.
Judy was beside him at once, hand feather-light on his
arm. "But what happened to you? Are you all right?"

"No," he said. He told her what had happened. As he
did she brought him fresh clothes, and he stood around on
the creek side of the wagon and changed as he told the
story.

"I hope you killed some of them," she said savagely,
after he'd finished recounting the assault.

"So did I—at first. Then I realized that if I had, they'd

be playing for keeps from here on." He told the rest, of his awakening at the Silvers, and what he had learned there.

"So Mr. Silver believes those men were murdered?"

Doc took the bottle of Egyptian Cure she had brought at his request and drained it, tipping his head back and pumping his Adam's apple up and down. "He's sure of it."

"Why?"

He lowered the bottle, shook his head, then shook all over. "Ah, that's better," he said.

Judy cocked her head. "Pardon my curiosity, but what's in that stuff, anyway?"

"Mostly laudanum."

She frowned. "Is it right for you to sell it to people as a cure-all?"

"Well, it *is* my cover, after all. But still, I think that there's a good deal to my Patented Egyptian Cure. It's my firm belief that most woes people suffer are caused by their own anxiety—they bring them on themselves, physical or mental. My Cure relaxes their minds and bodies and, I really believe, alleviates their suffering no matter what the nature of it." He shook his head. "But enough of that. You asked why Benjamin Silver thought those men were murdered. It's because they were meeting at the Ballenkamp place to discuss what was to be done about our Mr. Durán and his Forty Thieves. They had formed a sort of secret society."

"And how did Mr. Silver know all this?" Judy asked, a trifle skeptically.

"He was the fifth member of their council. Sixth, if you count Mr. Ballenkamp, who knew what was going on and approved. He had a fever that night and Deborah wouldn't let him out of the house."

"Oh." Judy looked stricken at the thought of how narrowly the old merchant had escaped death. "And he wanted you to go to the territorial government with the story?"

"Apparently that was what the Roadhouse Council—as they called it—had decided on. All except for our friend Odelbert, of the S.W.S.C. *He* wanted to fight it out." Doc frowned and rubbed his chin. A bluish stubble had sprouted on it. He had an extremely dark beard, especially for a man as fair as he was. "Seemed to me that someone else did too—someone not part of the council. But old Silver scooted over the subject. And his daughter didn't elaborate either."

"Was she pretty?" Judy asked out of the blue.

"Uh, er—well, the truth is, I didn't notice. I wasn't in much shape to, and it was dark." He didn't look at his fellow agent, but he sensed she wasn't buying it. *He* wouldn't have. *Why am I lying to her?* he asked himself.

He switched the subject. "Silver's story doesn't constitute proof—none that would stand up in court," he said. He was feeling better already, warm and sort of rosy. Let Judy scoff all she wanted—his Egyptian Cure *worked,* and he would peddle it with redoubled fervor tonight. If anyone showed up.

"I do feel that it fairly confirms the South-Western Stage Company suspicions," he continued. "All we need now is some solid proof."

He stood up and stretched. "Well, I guess we'd best be getting the tent set up," he said. "The show must go on."

Judy winced at the hoary cliché. "How do we go about getting our proof?"

"We don't," he said. "That's Raider's job."

"Hey! You! Cut out that racket in there!" The stocky turnkey with the belly on him that made him look as if he'd swallowed a cannonball rapped his billy club against the bars of Raider's cell.

"We *are* a band of brothers, *native* to the soil . . ." The tall, lean Pinkerton lay on his back on his bed, which was a wooden shelf clamped to the wall on one side and supported by chains at the other, with a thin pallet stuffed with straw for padding. His Stetson was down over his eyes, and his fingers were knotted over his flat belly. He was singing grandly and unself-consciously off-key, as if he didn't have a care in the world.

"Shut up, y'hear me, boy?" The guard rapped again, clacking the club rapidly back and forth between two bars.

Raider stopped his song and cocked an eye at the pot-gutted jailor. "Fuck you, Sarge," he said cheerfully.

The guard's heavy face turned crimson. He swelled up, a vein throbbing dangerously in his forehead, beneath the widow's peak of his close-cropped iron-gray hair. "You can't talk to me like that, you bum!" he roared.

"Who the hell says I can't, you hang-bellied Yankee sonovabitch," Raider replied.

"You—you—" With trembling hand he raised his bunch of keys and tried to fit one in the lock of Raider's cell. He couldn't seem to fit the key in the hole, which made him madder still. "I'll teach you to talk back to me, you polecat!"

"Yeah," Raider sneered. He pulled himself up on one elbow and pushed his hat up out of his eyes. "Why don't you? Come on along in here, Sarge. I'll shove that little stick so far up your ass you'll gag on it. Or mebbe you won't. You're prob'ly used to that sort of thing from Broward—not that he's got enough to push far past your asshole. Either asshole—the one in your pants or the one beneath your nose."

The turnkey was just standing outside the cell quivering with rage. His face and hands, every skin left visible by his flannel shirt and baggy corduroy trousers, glowed a red so hot Raider expected his clothing and sparse hair to start smoldering at any second. *He gits any madder, he gon' bust somethin'*, Raider observed, with keen interest.

It was unkind of Raider to ride the jailer, he knew. And maybe pushing his luck—but just a little. He knew that any man of the Las Peñas police force, up to Chief Broward, he guessed, would die before permitting any permanent harm to come to him. Because if any did they'd be liable to die a lot slower. He doubted they'd let any harm at all come to him, even from being bounced off the walls a bit, in accordance with the standard police procedures of the day.

Of course, Jailer Adams might just let his fury get the better of him, and come in to teach the saucy prisoner a few lessons in jailhouse decorum. But Raider had promised what would happen if he tried. And he meant to deliver on that promise.

He hoped he wouldn't have to, though. That would commit him to breaking jail. And that, at the moment, was the last thing Raider wanted.

Adams's trembling fit passed. He stood there, pale now, biting his lip fit to chomp it off. "I'll fix you," he said in a shaky voice. "We ain't supposed to let anything happen to you. But someday—*someday* . . ."

Raider tipped his hat back over his eyes and picked up his song where he'd left off.

Adams stood there reciting a litany of abuse. "You scum. You skunk. You mother-humping puke. You sorry little piece of shit . . ."

"And hold aloft the bonny blue flag—"

"You fucker. You sheep fucker. You *goat* fucker . . ."

"Adams," a bull voice demanded, "just what in the name of hell is going on in here?"

"Cocksucker," hissed Adams, too caught up in what he was doing to hear.

"—that bears the single star!"

"*Adams!*" The walls reverberated to the roar.

The big-bellied jailor jumped like a scalded cat. He spun round in midair and came down facing the heavy door that led to the outer world, which he had left unlocked and which had been opened without his noticing. His face went dead white. "Ch-chief?"

Chief Broward stood there with his face rumpled like an angry bed and his hand on his hips. "Adams," he gritted, "you ever again fail to hop to it when I speak to you, I'm gonna take you and muck out them cells with your ugly mug. Now take your unsightly carcass somewhere the hell else, and make it snappy!''

Adams flattened himself against the wall—except for his kettle belly, which refused to cooperate. It stuck obstinately out as he tried to slink past his boss and out of the corridor. Broward stood there glowering and refused to step aside, with the result that the turnkey's prodigious gut hung up on his hip, wedging the unfortunate Adams between his superior and the door frame.

Broward jabbed Adams in the belly. The jailor's eyes practically popped out. ''You're a disgrace to the department!'' Broward screamed. ''Now *clear out*!''

The poke in the chitlins had at least enabled the turnkey to fit past his boss. Adams gibbered something unintelligible and disappeared.

Broward shook his big white-maned head. ''Damn. Don't know how I can be expected to keep the peace if that's all the better help I can get!''

He looked at Raider, the sole occupant of the cell block. Raider was still flat on his back, but his hat was up again. He had watched Adams's discomfiture with an interest as undisguised as his grin. ''That's all I got to do with my time,'' Broward grumbled. ''Put on a show for every grifter and drifter to blow in offa the Llano Estacado.'' He sighed gustily. ''Well, it's your lucky day, boy. Get up offa there and dust off your ass.''

''Why should I do that, now, Chief?'' Raider taunted.

Broward drew a deep breath and controlled himself with a visible effort. His self-control was a lot better than Adams's had been. '' 'Cause you're bein' bailed out,'' he said, ''and 'cause a gentleman stands when a lady comes into his presence. And by God, you'll act like a gentleman in my jail, no matter who—''

He prudently cut the flow of words off there and stepped to one side. Raider was on his feet and stretching like a waking cat when in walked Sancha Durán, looking cool and lovely and wicked in her tight blouse and riding breeches, wih a little flat-brimmed Andalusian hat tipped to one side of her head and a riding crop tucked under one arm. Raider suppressed the impulse to check his pocket watch and say, *You're late*.

"Afternoon, ma'am," he said, with just a touch of insolence. "You look mighty purty today."

A warning growl came from somewhere deep in Chief Broward's barrel chest. But Sancha smiled, her yellow eyes glowing like a schoolgirl's at the compliment. "Thank you, señor. You are looking remarkably fresh yourself, for one who has just passed a night in jail."

He stretched again, insouciantly. "'Twarn't much," he allowed. "The food'd gag a goat, of course. And a couple o' sowbelly cops took turns bangin' on me like I was a ol' kettledrum, just to show they could. But all that ain't nothin' to a man like me."

Both his listeners had gone white at his words. "Who laid hands on this man?" Sancha spat, rounding on Broward like a cougar.

The burly police chief was shaking in his black shoes. "Why, nobody, ma'am, he's lyin' through his teeth, we'd never—"

"*Callate!*" She raised her quirt as if to strike him. "Enough of your infantile lies! Tell me who it was, so I can see him crawl!"

"I—I—" Broward was babbling now, his blue eyes standing out from his head in sheer terror. He could have broken the slim *nativa* in half with his thick arms—but he couldn't have been more afraid of a grizzly bear rearing over him with six-inch claws poised to take off his head. *Interestin'*, Raider thought.

"You can lay off him, ma'am," he said softly. "I was just funnin'. They ain't touched me—guess I have you to thank fer that." He flashed his most ingratiating grin.

Broward's look promised him death by torture that would gag a Chiricahua, but Sancha threw back her head and laughed. "Oh! Are you not clever! I knew you were a real man."

Raider tried to look modest. Not hard. But he tried.

In short order he found himself released into the custody of Sancha Durán and riding down the street knee to knee with her. To his not very great surprise she was mounted on a gigantic stallion, midnight black, with a white blaze down his face. It was all Raider could do to keep his bay stud from going for the beast, and to keep his thigh out of range of the black's teeth without showing apprehension to Sancha. She was not looking for a sign of weakness in him just now.

"You were in a grave situation, my friend," she told him with a straight face as they passed out of town and caught the trail he had ridden with Redeye King two days before. "You faced charges of murder. It could have gone hard with you."

"Shot a man who threw down on me first," Raider said. "But I reckon that wouldn'ta mattered to a Las Peñas jury."

"My brother had to use all his considerable influence to have you set free," she said earnestly, ignoring Raider's remark. She said it with such conviction that he wondered if she were crazy enough to actually *believe* it. "But he wants very badly for you to come to work for him.

"Of course," she added, flashing him a scintillating smile, "I helped to convince my brother to intercede for you."

He grinned back. His cock ached with the wanting of her, and the look that passed between them when his eyes met hers told him she would not deny his desire.

He'd known since they'd clapped the irons on him at Ramona's how it would all turn out. It was neatly done but obvious—to his not inexpert eye, at least. Durán did want him badly; why, he couldn't quite tell. The master of the Forty Thieves had sent Rynerson off to call Raider out and kill him. But Durán had heard of, and possibly witnessed, what Raider did to the knife-fancying Díaz that day at the Castile, knew that Raider was deadly quick and accurate with a six-gun. Durán had figured Raider would take

Rynerson, who had probably proven himself expendable some way or another.

And if Rynerson won the face-off . . . well, Durán didn't want any second-raters working for him. And Raider wouldn't be trying to horn in on his territory anymore.

The way the police had turned up before the gunsmoke had blown clear of the muzzle of Raider's Remington had tipped the Pinkerton to the way the wind blew. The fact that they arrested him flat-out for murder, in as obvious a case of self-defense as he'd ever seen, had cinched it. For the first time in his life he had gone off to jail without having the sick fear in the pit of his stomach that he'd never see the outside of the walls again. He knew that the Forty Thieves were going to all this trouble to recruit him, and they wouldn't let him rot in jail—just let him stay long enough to get a taste of what would happen if he still tried to hold out.

In fact, had he had anyone to bet with, he'd have laid good money that it would be Sancha Durán who came to fetch him to his new home. He figured that mad-eyed Sancha had more than a little to do with the trouble her brother was going to on his behalf. How much—that was another question.

"You are a man of honor," Sancha asserted. They were climbing a twisting trail now, winding in and out among the reddish-boled long-needled ponderosas. "I could see that the moment I laid eyes on you. So now you understand that you are one of us—one of the Forty Thieves, as the vulgar call my brother's men."

"It's true," he said, rubbing his chin as though mulling this over. He had quite a growth of stubble on his face, thick and black and thorny. "It's a *pundonor* for me now." A point of honor.

Her face lit. "You do understand! And your Spanish is beautiful. Are you certain you are a gringo, señor? You could be one of us, with your beautiful looks, the way you speak our language, the way you carry yourself—the way you think."

She thinks she's payin' you a compliment, he reminded himself. "Don't rightly know," he said, smoothly shaping his role to fit new circumstances. "I come up in a orphanage, down in New Orleans. Never knowed who my parents was."

"New Orleans?" She raised a slender eyebrow. "There are many Spanish in New Orleans."

That's why I picked it, darlin'.

They rode for a while in silence. It was a beautiful spring day, with the sun shining brightly down through the branches. The air was invigorating, especially after the stink of the jail. Raider drank it down in huge gulping lungfuls.

They came to the top of a rise, dropped down into a saddle between heights. Sancha turned the black's nose to the left, heading off the trail into a small clearing without a look at Raider. He turned the bay to follow.

"This ain't the trail to the Castile," he said, catching her as she came to the trees at the bottom of the glade.

She reined in. "Are you in such a hurry to reach the hacienda, then?" she asked. Without waiting for a reply she dismounted.

His heart in his throat, Raider slipped off his horse. Sancha had her hat in one hand. The other was at the back of her neck, and as Raider watched she shook her hair free in a gleaming black cascade. He whistled appreciatively. The hair hung clear to her trim butt.

"I am beautiful, am I not?" she said.

"More beautiful than any woman I've knowed." It was true. Her standing there with her hair unbound and sunlight dappling it, slim and ready with her nipples standing in low relief against the thin fabric of her blouse, her lips red and moist and slightly forward, waiting for him—the sight was like a drug. He growled low in his throat and stepped forward, reaching for her.

"You're beautiful too," she said. He caught her shoulders, buried his face at the base of her throat, and kissed her with savage force. She laughed and skimmed the hat off into the scrub oak.

She reached down and caught a handful of his coarse, straight hair. She pulled hard, so hard tears sprang reflexively into Raider's eyes. He started to protest, but Sancha reached down her other hand and tore open her blouse. She yanked Raider's head to her small hard breast. He fastened his lips on the stiff brown nipple and sucked for all he was worth.

Still smarting over the way she'd pulled his hair, he bit down on the stiff nipple, lightly at first, then hard. Her breath hissed sharply over clenched teeth and her whip-lean body went rigid. *"Ah, sí, sí,"* she gasped. "Yes! Hurt me! *Hurt* me!"

He gnawed brutally at her tit, mauling the other with a hard hand. Her fingers caressed the back of his head and neck, crushing him against her. His free hand slid down her slim back, delved into her jeans. Her rump was hard and deliciously rounded in his hand. He slid it down further. He felt the coarse black tangle of her cunt, delved a finger into it. The fur was sopping wet. The finger probed, found rubbery, slippery lips, burrowed between.

Her body jerked. For a moment she canted her hips back and fucked herself on the intruding finger. She dropped her head and began to chew at the top of his skull. It was something no woman had ever done to Raider before. He found it wildly stimulating. It was like fucking some kind of animal, some untamed hunting she-cat. He knew now she'd leave claw marks on his back, and the thought drove him like a whip.

She let go of his head to tear at her breeches with hands turned to talons by lust. He let go of her tit and began fumbling with the buttons of her fly. She moaned and plunged a small cool hand down the front of his jeans. Her fingers found his cock, pumped it madly. He gasped around the succulent mouthful of her flesh.

Then he was sliding her riding breeches down her slender hips, and she was frantically pulling open the front of his pants. His cock sprang free and vibrated the way Miguelito's dagger had in the willow bole. Sancha kicked off her high boots and dragged her breeches off one-handed, using the other to keep Raider's head pinioned against her breast. He kept up his brutal assault, biting as hard as he could without drawing blood. He wasn't ready to go *that* far, even in his feeding-frenzy of lust—and he didn't know if she was either. He didn't even want to imagine the penalty for doing some sort of lasting damage to the crazy queen of Thieves.

His pants were down around his ankles. He scraped his boots off anywhichway and managed to pull one leg out of his drawers. That was enough for now—he had to plunge his manhood full-length into Sancha's waiting snatch or he'd blow off on her belly.

He had the measure of her now. He pried his head away from her tit and pressed his mouth to hers. Her tongue was down his throat at once like a blackfoot ferret down a prairie-dog hole. He glanced over her shoulder. There was the straight bole of a ponderosa not six feet behind her. He leaned into her, forcing her back. She resisted for a moment, drawing the head of his penis down into her bush. The friction almost drove him crazy.

He pushed the woman back until she fetched up against the tree. Her eyes flew open, staring madly into his with a bizarre admixture of need, fear, and supplication. "Yes," she breathed. "Take me now. Take me *hard*. Now!"

She raised a slim leg and cocked it around his waist. He felt her pussy kiss the head of his prick. He put one hand against the tree to brace him, grabbed her by the waist with the other, and thrust forward.

They cried out in unison as he sank full-length inside her. Her pussy sheath was unbelievably tight, virgin tight. The muscles of it played along his cock, teasing him, drawing him on. His tongue strove with hers. He rammed into her as hard as he could, driving her bare ass against the rough bark of the tree. He could feel the pleasure tingling in her like jolts of electricity, knew he had judged right.

He had scarcely started to pump her before he felt her tighten around him. He slid his hands up behind her back and gripped her shoulders, impaling her upon his thrusting cock. She moaned and writhed and clawed at his back, ripping the skin with her blood-red nails. He didn't even notice as his own orgasm overtook him like a flash flood.

Her cunt milked him dry. Her ass worked around and around, rubbing itself raw on the tree, swirling his dick inside her. The pleasure went on and on until it became pain, became unendurable.

He tried to draw away. She wouldn't let him. Her leg became a band of iron around his waist, her fingers hooks digging deep into his flesh. He felt an irrational surge of panic—recalled the legend of La Lorona, the demon who enticed men to her bower and used them and used them till there was nothing left but empty husks.

Her eyes found his and challenged him. *Are you afraid?* they asked tauntingly. *If you are, I shall destroy you. I shall use you up and cast you aside, because you are not man enough for me.*

For the first time in his life, he sensed, his life depended on his ability to take up her sexual challenge. He forced the fear from him. In its wake came a fresh wave of pleasure as her skilled cunt played on his cock.

He dropped his head to the juncture of neck and shoulder and began to nibble her sweat-tangy olive skin. His hips resumed the rhythm of fucking. Again she hauled him rudely back by the hair. "No," she said hoarsely.

He frowned. *Is she tryin' to tease me?* It made no sense.

Her leg slipped from around his waist. He literally would have fallen over backwards if his cock hadn't been buried hilt-deep in her belly. She eeled out from between him and the pine. He made a small childish sound of disappointment as her pussy slipped off his once-more rampant cock.

For a moment she stood admiring his cock. It was big and thick and glistening with their mingled juices. Sancha dropped to her knees and engulfed the swollen purple head with her mouth. Raider gasped and threw his head back. His knees went watery.

Turnabout seemed the name of the game. He grabbed a double handful of her hair and twisted. She moaned around his dick and writhed in apparent delight. He began to haul her head roughly back and forth, fucking her face with savage force.

She endured this for a moment—more than endured, with her tongue twining like a serpent around his prick. Then she tore away, leaving long black strands of hair hanging from his clenched fists. He stared at her in wonder and admiration. She was crazier than a pet coon, but there was something purely magnificent about her, all the same.

She turned from him and dropped to her hands and knees. She reached a slim hand back for him. He knelt behind her, grabbed his prick, and steered it toward the slightly slackened lips of her sex.

Her hand intercepted his cock. "No—*here*." She redirected his throbbing organ to the tight pucker of her anus.

He blinked in surprise. He wasn't used to this sort of thing, not hardly. Before he could pull away, she had relaxed her sphincter and driven herself back, impaling herself on his dick. "My *God!*" he breathed. Her ass was incredibly tight, so tight as to be painful to his blood-gorged member.

But pleasure from pain seemed the order of the day. While he was frozen by surprise she began to pump herself back and forth, her knees crackling on the fallen triple clusters of needles, her fingers teasing his balls. In a matter of moments he had forgotten all about surprise and pain both, and began pumping his prick enthusiastically in and out of her asshole.

Her butt cheeks were exquisitely formed. The rubbing against the bark of the pine tree had given them a kind of rosy blush that Raider found erotic. *Maybe this crazy woman ain't so crazy after all.* She had certainly showed him a side to sex he had never even dreamed existed.

He rested his hands on her lovely chafed ass. It was a pleasure watching his cock disappear up her back and reappear again—almost as much as the feel of her unbelievable tightness swallowing him up.

She began to moan, low in her throat, catlike, wanton, urgent. His fingers dug into the tender flesh of her ass as his own passion built inexorably toward a new explosion. "Ah, yes, yes," she howled. "Hard, hard. Be hard! Be brutal! Make me *scream!*"

He did his best. He piled into her with all the force he could muster, bringing her knees off the duff with each thrust. She squealed and wagged her rump. He thought the top of his head would come off.

At the last moment she plunged a hand into the black thatch between her groin, sank fingers deep into her cunt. She began to scream, loud and high and long, and then he was crying out, exploding into her, pumping his seed frantically into her rectum from a cock rubbed raw by unbearable friction.

Her arms gave way and she went face-first into the fragrant carpet of fallen pine needles. He collapsed atop her. His prick slid out of her butt, trailing a trickle of come onto her satin thigh. She rolled onto her back and her hands stole around his neck as she began to nibble her way up his throat.

By Jesus, he thought. *The woman ain't finished yet!*

He'd always known he might not survive this mission. That was the chance you always took.

But somehow I never thought I might cash it in this way!

CHAPTER NINE

"Doctor." It was Judy's voice from the streambank. Doc looked up from where he was seated in the box of the wagon, encrypting a report for the Chicago office of the Pinkertons. "There's someone coming."

He reached down instinctively. The reassuring cool solidity of the shotgun was there, just beside the seat. Good. He had no wish to be caught flat-footed again.

He looked out across the field. Someone was walking forward through broad patches of white wildflowers that looked like milk spilled on the dusty green grass. A female someone by the looks, tall and slender, wearing a bonnet. She had on a light gray dress with a white collar. Not a very springlike outfit, but the walk was young. Doc's heart sped up. *Could it be . . .?*

"Dr. Weatherbee?" asked Deborah Silver in her quiet voice as she came within earshot of the wagon. Judith raised her head, appraised the newcomer, snorted, and went back to grazing. It was the closest thing to approval the mule ever offered. "May I speak with you a moment?"

Judy was coming back from the stream, carrying two full buckets of water. She eyed the newcomer warily. "Teresa," Doc called. "There's someone I'd like you to meet. This is Deborah Silver. She and her father took me in and tended to me yesterday, after those ruffians jumped me."

Judy came up and set her buckets down next to the

offside rear wheel. "I'm pleased to meet you," she said in a neutral tone. "I'm obliged to you for helping the doctor. I don't know what I'd do without him."

This little protestation of feminine helplessness rang jarringly false in Doc's ears. He guessed Judy thought it was in character—unless the little bitch was having a little sarcastic fun at his expense. "Uh, Deborah, meet Teresa, my assistant. She's an invaluable helper; I don't know what I'd do without *her*, either."

Both women favored him with brief looks that told him he was being banal and everybody knew it. "The pleasure is mine," Deborah said. "Please forgive me for taking the doctor away from you for a time but . . . but I must speak with him."

Judy smiled. It never touched her eyes. "Go right ahead. I've got chores around camp to tend to. Why don't you walk down by the stream? It's very pleasant today." She cast Doc a bleak look.

"Thank you," Deborah said. "You're very thoughtful."

She and Doc walked down to the stream, then turned right and began to stroll along the bank. Doc could see a shoal of tiny fishes hovering like a cloud in the water by the shore. They gave the illusion of following the pair. He guessed they were just seeing different schools, or different bits of the same school, that seemed by some trick of light to be following them.

"What's on your mind, Deborah?" he asked when they were well out of earshot of the camp. He had the distinct impression that Judy was watching, though when he looked up at the wagon she was nowhere in sight. Drat her anyway.

"I—I've come to talk about what my father asked you to do yesterday."

He sucked on his upper lip. "Well, I've been thinking about it, and—"

"Oh, you must not!" She clutched his arm. "You can't do what he asks! It would destroy you both."

He broke stride and almost lost his balance. "What on earth do you mean?"

"Durán has friends in Santa Fe. What will happen when you arrive with a petition asking the governor to send troops to pull down Durán and that fine house of his?" She stopped and faced him, lovely face upturned, liquid eyes pleading. "My father escaped death once by sheerest accident. If Durán finds out he is still working against him . . . this time there will be no escape."

Doc put his hands gently on her shoulders, then quickly removed them. The contact with her skin was electric. He looked into her eyes, but she looked away. *Did she feel it too? Or am I letting my romantic nature get the better of me?*

"I had already decided not to honor your father's request," he said, with just the slightest catch in his voice. She was very beautiful, standing there with her face upturned to him in the warm morning sunlight. He had to battle the urge to kiss those full lips. "It was very hard for me. I'm indebted to him. As I am to you."

She squeezed his hands. "Oh, thank you." She suddenly leaned forward and kissed his cheek. "This means so much to me. And to my brother."

"Your brother? I don't believe I met him."

She looked away. "He doesn't come to the house anymore," she all but whispered. "He cannot."

"But why not?"

"Because he's wanted for murder." The words were scarcely audible above the sounds of the stream and the wind.

Doc blinked. He sent a nervous glance toward the wagon, now a hundred yards distant. Still no sign of Judy. He took hold of Deborah's arm and began to walk her along the stream again. It was a minute or two before he could find words.

"Tell me about it."

She bit her lip. "There's not much to tell. My brother David is two years older than I am, twenty." *Strange*, Doc thought. *I didn't think she was so young.* "He's very headstrong, and very, very protective of me." She smiled shyly up at him.

"I can see how he would be."

"Henry Durán decided that he . . . liked me. He came around several times, but Father would never let him see me. Nor would I have!" Anger flared up in her, hot and bright. It was gone like the flash of a match. "He sent men for me. One day while I was at market. One man, named Saiz, I believe, grabbed me and tried to pull me across his saddle. It was near my father's store. David was in the front room at the time; he saw it happen through the window. He grabbed a rifle, ran out, and shot the man through the head. I fell back. The other two rode their horses at me. David shot at them, wounded one, and both fled.

"Soon after that policemen came with a warrant for David's arrest. It's murder for a brother to protect his sister from rape. Did you know that? At least that's the way it is in Las Peñas," she said bitterly.

"I'm sorry," Doc said lamely.

"Father—" She choked. "Father wanted David to surrender. He said that it was wrong that David had spilled a man's blood, but that God would forgive him since he was young. But he had to give himself up! My father said that he knew that the truth would come out, that justice would be served." Her face was stark. "So long has he lived; so little has he learned!"

"What happened?"

"David fled into the mountains. Posses hunted for him. Some of them were not so eager to find him, I think. Not everyone was sorry to see one of the Forty Thieves lying dead in the street. But others—others would have been only too glad to help run the dirty Jew-boy into the ground."

Doc took her in his arms and folded her to his chest. It was a strong, deep chest, and she seemed to like it there. He could think of nothing to say, so he merely stroked her glossy dark hair where her blue bonnet had fallen askew.

Then, slowly, it came to him. "Deborah," he said softly. "Do you think it would be possible for me to meet your brother?"

She drew back and looked up at him. Hope and suspicion mingled in her expression. "Why?"

He took a deep breath. "Have you ever heard of the Pinkerton National Detective Agency?" he asked.

Sunlight filtered in through pale chintz curtains and began to creep up Raider's face. When it reached his eyes he stirred, muttered to himself, and came awake. He sat up and looked around the small room with the *vigas* overhead.

A moment of disorientation. Then the thought: *Wherever I am, it's a damn sight better than the Las Peñas jail.*

Then it came back to him. He dropped back on the pillow, a smile on his face. He was in with the Forty Thieves—and Sancha Durán.

It had been late afternoon when the pair had finally ridden in through the double gates of the Castile ranch house—sweaty, happy, and sexually replete. Durán himself had been standing in the *portal* to greet them, looking cool and pulled-together as usual in his elegantly cut rancher's clothes.

He had shaken Raider's hand with his cool dry grip. "Welcome to El Castilla," he said warmly. "I am glad you have decided to join us after all." And placing his hand on Raider's shoulder, he had ushered the tall Pink into the cool dimness of his house as if he intended to make him a permanent fixture.

"Allow me to be the first to congratulate you on the successful outcome of your brush with the law," Durán said, showing his even teeth in a smile. "You are a very fortunate fellow. These provincial courts can be quite arbitrary with outsiders."

Raider thanked him, thinking, *Christ, but I'd hate to play poker with the little fuck.*

If there was a slightly unreal quality to his welcome to the stronghold of the Forty Thieves, things quickly became outright eerie. He was to be quartered in the main house—no bedding down in the bunkhouse with the rabble for him. They even had what kit he had to his name, tucked away neatly in one of the seemingly myriad bedrooms on the ground floor of the sprawling villa. Some Thieves had obviously been dispatched to pick it up from his hotel— quite possibly even before the gunfight with Rynerson.

Durán had introduced him to his lieutenants: Dominguín, Grant Largo, and Augustín Álarid. They seemed guarded, and for his part Raider was content to dispense plain civility. The fact was, the names were familiar to him, except for Álarid's, and Raider was dying to wire back to Chicago for a dossier on him. Durán had recruited some really first-rate talent, and Raider was frankly flattered to have been chosen, the more so since Durán plainly intended him to take his place among the first rank of Thieves.

Lastly Raider met Marcosio Abadón. In a way the man was a disappointment. He was every bit as huge—and hideous—as he was made out to be; it looked as if someone had given his face a good working-over with a garden hoe. But the monstrous killer proved to be soft-spoken and mild, speaking good English with a border accent. The perfection of his teeth were jarring in that brutal parody of a face, but what *did* get to Raider was Abadón's eyes. They were like tiny anthracite beads, glittering with intelligence and malice. Raider was no sophisticate, but he was a solid judge of character—otherwise he'd have fetched up dead the first time he tried to swing a role for Allan Pinkerton. And he got the uneasy feeling that Abadón's storied sadism was not the unthinking reflex of a brute, but a studied policy. Calculated terrorism. Suddenly he felt cold sweat break out all over his body, and he thought, *Yeah, the things they say about him are true—as far as they go.*

But I got the feelin' they don't tell the half of it.

After meeting the big shots Raider got a tour of the ranch. He met a number more of his fellow Thieves, who by and large seemed more reserved around him than Durán's lieutenants. Most he'd never heard of, men with names like Bennett Wix, Ygnacio Sandoval, Onofre Baca, Miguel Leyba. Others he knew of, either professionally or from Redeye's stories: Slowhand McVie, baby-faced, towheaded, and in his own way as crazy as Sancha Durán; Isham Lee, a trim dark-skinned black noted for his proficiency with a scatter-gun; Toby Sublette with his pit bull eyes; Cesario Blea, a walking mound of muscle with a little curl in the middle of his forehead like the girl in the story. There were some he'd met with Redeye: whitehaired Curly Snow, stumpy Claude Baker the blaster, cockeyed Miguelito Diaz, who eyed him the way a cat watches a bird through a glass window. And here came Redeye himself, redder of eye and more redolent of cheap hooch than usual, to slobber over Raider his joy that his good buddy had seen the light at last.

Dinner was strangest of all. He would dine with the master in the main house, he was informed by Pedro, the majordomo, a snotty little Indian, almost black, who looked exactly like Benito Juárez; normally, formal attire was demanded, but Mr. Raider would be excused until he provided himself with proper dress.

The next thing he knew he was sitting at a huge table under an immense black wrought-iron chandelier, surrounded by people dressed as if they were attending the President's inauguration. At the head of the table sat Durán, decked out in stand-up collar and black swallowtail coat, like a New Orleans swell from the forties, with a red cummerbund around his slim waist. On his right sat sister Sancha, looking regal in a long black dress that clung to her like skin and displayed her small bosom to maximum effect. Her hair was caught atop her head with a heavy black barrette. Her lips were painted blood red. She gave Raider a sidelong glance when Pedro squired him in, and ran her tongue around her lips. *Jesus,* he thought.

On Durán's left sat Sallee LaSalle, resplendent in a dress of shimmering green silk that left very little of her remarkable snow-white breasts to the imagination. Her hair was piled in a golden confection atop her head, with of all things a diamond tiara topping the whole thing off, and another string of gaudy sparklers around her neck. They looked real to Raider, who had an eye as practiced as any jewel thief; testimony to the personal power of Henry Durán that none of his merry band had slit that lovely white throat one night to make away with all that ice.

The lieutenants were there: the tall cadaverous Larkin Hanks, a dour Puritan fanatic who should have ridden with Cromwell, whom everyone called the Preacher, with mad black eyes set either side of a blade of a nose, a bristling black beard, lank hair combed across the balding crown of his head; Grant Largo, medium height, light of build, languid of manner, the American-born bastard of an Italian count and an English gentlewoman, with a pale face, dark eyes with slight puffy lids, neat brown hair, and a meticulously tended beard and mustache; the unknown Álarid, a plump and jovial man in tight black jacket and pants and red sash, looking like a bandmaster from Jalisco; and finally Dominguín. The sometime guerrilla didn't look like a notorious revolutionary and impaler; he was tall and lean except for a little potbelly pushing out the ruffled front of his white shirt, with a long, sad face, sensitive intelligent dark eyes, hawk nose, droopy mustache, and a high balding dome of a head. With his long thin soft-looking hands he looked like a concert violinist—maybe in Augustín Álarid's band.

Dinner passed in a haze of unreality. Raider was able to gather that something big was in the wind, and more than once Durán hinted that his chance to prove himself would come before he knew it. Sancha kept giving him looks that had his crotch in an uproar, for all that his cock felt as if she'd been at it with sandpaper from the afternoon's activities. He noticed Sallee was looking at him with more than a casual interest too, and he made it a point to smile at her, whenever Sancha's gimlet eyes weren't fixed on him. There was something more than coquetry in her heavily made up blue eyes: a hint of pleading, of urgency.

One thing Raider was thankful for was the absence of Marcosio Abadón from the affair. The spectacle of him decked out in a tailcoat and fancy sash with a silk rag knotted around his oak-trunk neck would have been just too much for Raider's nervous system.

After dinner Sallee and Sancha excused themselves, and brandy and cigars made the rounds—Raider declining the latter, and suffering in silence as the others puffed their stogies. He could never abide cigar smoke, and for a while it was touch and go whether he was going to be able to keep the fancy French-style cooking he'd been served on the inside of him.

They broke up at ten, Durán explaining that he kept rancher's hours and suggesting Raider get a good sleep. "Tomorrow is a busy day for you," he remarked, and disappeared. Raider was only to happy to drag himself to his room and collapse into the sybaritic softness of a featherbed. He'd put in a downright busy day today, and the shelf in the city jail where he'd spent the night before had not been what he'd call restful.

He had just drifted into the nothingness of sleep when the door opened. In a moment Sancha joined him in bed, lithe and eager as a mink in a lacy black negligee. Lord, what that woman couldn't do. What that woman *wouldn't* do!

Eventually she'd left him and stolen back to her own room, causing him to wonder if old Henry had any glimmering of his sister's real interest in the new arrival. He didn't wonder hard. He felt as if he'd been used as a paving stone for the Chisholm Trail for a whole year. He was asleep before the flitting black flame that was Sancha Durán was all the way out the door.

Normally he awoke at dawn. From the slant of the light through his window, he judged he'd missed that by a spell. He rose, stretched, felt himself. He had a funny floating feeling, and there were scratches all over his back, belly, and thighs—had she actually worn spurs to bed, or was that his imagination?—but nothing seemed to have been jarred loose. He dressed and wandered back to the kitchen, where the silent Pueblo woman fed him black coffee and *huevos rancheros,* which were almost as good as Ramona's—and that was saying some.

Feeling restored as he always did after getting himself around some good green chili, he strolled out the front of the big house and stood blinking into the midmorning sunlight.

A handful of Thieves were strewn around the packed-earth yard, on the portal and under the trees. Hostility struck him in the face like a panful of boiling water. The men stared slit-eyed at him for a moment, then edged away.

Well, there ain't nothin' like havin' your buddies take you to their bosom, he told himself. "Hey there, Curly," he called to the white-haired man, who was cleaning his rebored Colt Old Army. "Why the long face this fine mornin'?"

The old man looked at him with hatred bleak in his winter-gray eyes. He spat deliberately. The spittle rolled itself into a dustball between the toes of Raider's boots. The old man turned away.

"Friendly bunch of fellers," Raider commented. He started walking across the yard.

"Mr. Raider." He turned. Sallee LaSalle stood in the doorway behind him in an airy-looking white cotton dress. He grinned and tipped his hat to her.

"How are you this morning, miss?" he asked.

She bit her lip. "I'm fine," she said, in a way that made him know she wasn't. "Are you busy?"

"Don't have no duties yet. Just thought I'd walk, enjoy the good Lord's sunshine."

"May I walk with you?"

In answer he crooked an arm. She beamed and came to him, opening a yellow parasol with white fringe over her head, and slipped her arm through his. They walked arm in arm through the gates, chatting about nothing in particular.

As soon as they were out of the courtyard Sallee looked at him, her normally pink cheeks drained of all color. "Mr. Raider," she said hesitantly, "I have a feeling about you. I don't know if it's ridiculous or not—it seems to be—but then, my—my hunches are seldom wrong."

He felt an eager tightening in the pit of his belly, and didn't know whether it was professional interest or purely sex. But this beautiful buxom blonde was about to say something of import, he knew it.

Instead she went rigid. "There!" She flung out a white-gloved hand.

A black horse was loping across the broad valley toward the villa, a slim figure straight in the saddle on its back. "He's puttin' up an almighty cloud of dust," Raider commented. "Looks like he's dragging something."

Sallee's arm snaked out of Raider's. "Sancha's powerful jealous," she said. "If she sees . . ." She didn't need to finish the sentence.

The black stud was cutting overland, ignoring the broad road. Raider heard noises behind him, glanced back. A dozen or so Thieves had drifted out of the courtyard and stood silently behind him, grim death on their faces.

The horse was getting closer. Raider felt the eagerness in his belly turn to a lump of sick anticipation. His Indian-keen senses told him there was something violently, horribly wrong about this situation, but he couldn't put a finger on it to save him.

He heard measured footfalls on caliche and turned back again to see Durán standing there with his face shaded by a brown Stetson and his hands on his hips. Marcosio Abadón stood behind him like a gigantic shadow. Raider nodded to his new employer. Durán favored him with a tight, distracted smile and looked off at the approaching horse and rider. The giant's face was as unreadable as the granite outcrops overlooking the passes into Las Peñas.

Sallee screamed, a raw rising sound in the mellow breezy morning.

Raider spun round. Sancha Durán's big stud was dragging something behind it—a bulky, shapeless, flaccid thing, red-smeared. Something about the cast of it made Raider's stomach turn over.

Sancha sent the black trotting past the onlookers and performed a caracole. Sallee's shriek rose to an insane crescendo as the weighty object behind the horse bumped over a tuft of grass and into view. It was a man—what was left of him—who had had his hands tied behind him and been dragged for a few miles across the broken meadowland at the tail of Sancha's horse.

The face was a ghastly ruin. But enough remained to recognize the wattled gray jaws and one imploring red eye that had once belonged to Clarence King.

Sallee went to her knees, then toppled to the side, unconscious. Raider knelt by her. He looked up at Sancha Durán with loathing plain on his hawk face. But her head was in the air, the flush of sexual arousal glowing on her thin cheeks.

At a sign from Durán, Abadón came forward, stooped, and picked up Sallee LaSalle as if she were a doll. Durán came forward, shaking his head thoughtfully. "A pity," he murmured. "But it had to be done. Clarence drank too much; he had been warned what would happen if he failed again." He shook his head. "A distasteful matter, but discipline must be maintained."

He put his hand on Raider's shoulder. Raider could not remember a thing he'd done that was harder than not flinching away. "Come inside, Raider. We've important matters to discuss." A rare grin lit up his pockmarked features.

"Today we make the final plans to twist the tail of that wicked old Jew Silver. He won't be so eager to sabotage us when we have that daughter of his as our hostage!"

CHAPTER TEN

Pine branches rattled around the small clearing as the wind questing through the mountains shook them. "My sister said you wanted to meet me," David Silver said.

Doc nodded. He stood for a moment with the wind whipping his pants legs about his calves, sizing the young man up. David Silver was a handsome young man, not tall, with a compact build and a nervous wound-up manner that kept him rocking on the balls of his feet as if with impatience. He had a thin handsome face, a thin beak of a nose, gray eyes like his father's, but fiercer, more intense. Unruly coarse brown hair blew in the wind. He wore a vest, white shirt, jeans, boots, and a gunbelt. His horse, a black and white paint, was tethered to a tree a little bit behind him. A Winchester hung in a scabbard by the saddle horn.

Aware of the young man returning his scrutiny, Doc said, "Yes, I did. I'm from the Pinkerton National Detective Agency. You've heard of them?" A terse nod. "We're investigating the alleged murder of Mr. James Odelbert, late line manager for the South-Western Stage Company."

David Silver uttered a short bark of laughter. "There's no alleged about it, Dr. Weatherbee. It was murder."

He glanced at his sister, who stood by holding the bridle of her gray mare. "When are the troops arriving?"

Doc frowned. "I beg your pardon?"

"My father." David's smile was bitter and attenuated.

"Hasn't he convinced you to go to the authorities with his tales of conspiracy?"

"If he had, would I be here?" Doc asked. The younger man shook his head. "I take it you don't believe in this 'conspiracy.' "

"Oh, no, Doctor. I do. But I think it extends a lot farther upward than my father is willing to acknowledge. That's why I think the old fool is killing himself if he goes to Santa Fe."

"David!" cried Deborah, scandalized. "You're talking about our father."

"You know it's true." She dropped her eyes. David turned back to the chubby Pink, put his gloved hands on his hips, and looked him challengingly in the eye. "What are you going to do about Henry Durán and his Forty Thieves, Mr. Pinkerton?"

"First we need proof."

David laughed. "For what? To take to Santa Fe to be filed away somewhere while Durán grinds us into the mud? For God's sake, man, why not *act?*"

"We will," Doc said firmly, "as soon as we have our proof."

David shook his head. "My foolish sister has wasted both our time bringing you here," he said. "Good-bye, Doctor."

"You don't understand. My partner and I are collecting evidence now. It's our job. And we can't act without the evidence. But once we get the evidence—"

"You'll move?" Eagerly, leaning forward so far Doc feared he'd overbalance.

"Yes."

For a moment David Silver stood poised there. Then he drew back and shook his head. "Not good enough."

"And just why the hell not?" asked Doc in exasperation.

"The Forty Thieves are planning something big. They want to follow up their little performance at Hugo's with a real spectacular."

"I'd think the murder of seven—eight—people was spectacular enough."

"No way. Nobody saw it. There was no object lesson there—just bits of bodies strewn across the landscape. No, Durán is going to give the people of Las Peñas a show they'll never forget—those who survive."

"How do you know this, David?" Deborah asked.

"I have ways. I'm not the only man in Las Peñas with the nerve to stand up to the Thieves, thank God. I've got quite a little network a-building."

And you're just a bit jealous of the Pinks coming in and stealing your thunder. "That will be helpful when the time comes to move."

"If you ever decide to."

"We will. And we'll need you."

David's expression was skeptical. "You know where to find me. No, I'm not being foolhardy. But if you ride up the same way Deborah brought you today, I'll see you and meet up with you, once I'm satisfied you haven't been followed."

Doc offered his hand. David either didn't see it or chose to ignore it. He turned away, untethered his paint, and swung up into the saddle. "Something to keep under your hat," he said. "Time's getting very short. Durán's just picked himself up a new man who's supposed to be greased lightning with a gun. Lanky man, dark, with a black mustache like a Mexican bandit. Heard he didn't come cheap—and Durán's going to be in a hurry to put that expensive new talent to work." He wheeled the horse and rode downslope, into the trees. They watched him cross the gray stone of a dry streambed, and then he was gone.

Doc felt Deborah's hand on his arm. The contact felt good. "It's getting late," she said. "We should be on our way."

He nodded and started trudging up the grassy slope to where Judith was tied.

•   •   •

"Would you care to come in, Doctor?" Deborah asked as they turned into the alley behind the two-story house in which she lived with her father, "It'll take me just a second to put Sheba away. I can rub her down later. Let me get you a cup of tea first."

Doc glanced at the sun, sinking toward the Moscas in the west. The light had gone butter-colored, but he estimated that it was better than an hour till full dark. That gave him some leeway before he had to be back for the show. "I'd be honored."

Deborah dismounted. She was wearing a long gray woolen skirt and blouse and looked very fetching. She pulled her sidesaddle off expertly before Doc could even tender an offer of assistance. In short order Sheba was in her stall next to Benjamin Silver's old chestnut gelding in the little barn out behind the house, and Judith was tied outside with her face contentedly buried in a feed-bag.

The house was dark when they came in through the rear into the kitchen. Doc was surprised. "Where's your father?"

"He's at the store," Deborah replied. "He won't be home until several hours after dark." She struck a match and lit a lantern on the table. "Let me get a light on in the sitting room. Then I'll make the tea."

She led him into the sitting room, a small tidy room with a sofa, several understuffed chairs, and shelves crowded with books. He looked around as she lit several more lamps and returned to the kitchen. There were several photographs in frames on the wall. Doc found himself drawn to one, an ancient daguerreotype above the mantel. "This couldn't be you?"

She stuck her head out. "Beg pardon?"

He nodded. "You're not old enough for this to be you, are you?"

She dropped her eyes and wiped her hands on a cloth. "That's—that's my mother. She died when I was five."

"Oh." It seemed asinine to apologize for the death of a woman thirteen years ago, so Doc didn't say "I'm sorry."

He studied the picture. He could see where Deborah had

got her exotic Levantine looks. Mrs. Silver's face was a little rounder than her daughter's, and there was a touch of gray at the temples of her dark luxurious hair. But the high cheekbones, the huge almond eyes, the nose that managed to be assertive without overpowering, the intelligence and quiet humor of her expression—all these belonged to mother and daughter alike.

"She was very beautiful," Doc said. A pause. "Much like you."

She had come back with a little flowered white ceramic teapot and two cups on a tray. "Thank you," she said quietly, as she knelt to set the tray on a small table.

Doc came over and sat on the sofa. He accepted a tea-cup, poured in milk and a liberal amount of sugar. "You're a fascinating man, Doctor," Deborah said, sitting next to him. He raised an eyebrow. "My father says you're just a—a mountebank. I hope you don't think harshly of him."

Doc managed a wan laugh. "I can see how he'd be of that opinion."

She touched his hand. "Oh, but he likes you. He respects you. He has great respect for learning, and you're obviously a well-educated man. 'Such a nice young man, well-mannered, very bright. Why can't he find something useful to do with his life?' That's what he says." She was avoiding his gaze.

"He sounds a lot like my father," Doc admitted.

She laughed, gently. Impulse made him reach out, take her chin, and turn her face gently to his. "What do *you* think of me? Struck by the impulse to reform?"

She shook her head. "I think I like you the way you are—however you choose to be."

He kissed her.

For a moment she resisted. Then her lips parted. She set down her teacup and placed her hands behind his neck. Her fingers caressed the back of his head lightly.

They broke apart. Her eyes and lips were shining. "I love your hair," she said. "So soft. So fair."

He reached up and pulled the pins from her hair. "I like yours, too."

She studied him for a moment. Her small pink tongue peeked briefly between her lips. Then she seized his hand with sudden resolution. "Come."

He followed her, up the narrow stairs to a familiar-looking bedroom. She led him inside and shut the door behind. It was dark in the room, little light coming through the curtains from the twilit street. She took him to the bed, pushed him till he sat.

She stood back. She reached toward the front of her blouse, slowly undid the buttons. Her eyes were fixed on his. The blouse fell open. Her breasts were large and full and lovely. Broad areolae and erect thick nipples were the color of wine. She placed the blouse on a dresser, unfastened her skirt and removed that, then stepped gracefully out of her frilly underthings. Her body was gorgeous, even in the half-light. Her legs were slender and strong, hips generous, as was the dark wedge of hair between her smooth thighs. Her belly was a firm low dome.

She knelt on the bed at Doc's side. Reverently he cradled one breast, raised it to his lips to kiss the nipple. The taste of her was salty-sweet.

She untied his necktie. Reluctantly he relinquished her breast and started helping with his own clothes. *There are some disadvantages to being a model of sartorial perfection,* he thought wryly.

But soon he was naked with her. He took her in his arms and laid her gently back upon the counterpane. She gazed up at him with those lovely oriental eyes half-lidded and serene.

"Love me," she said.

He pressed his palm to her pubic mound. The fur was crisp and curly. Her hips began to move sinuously as he massaged her breast and cunt. His tongue traced the outline of her lips. Her fingers played with the hair at the back of his head.

He ran a finger up the lips of her vagina. She tensed,

arching her back. He kissed her lips, slipped his finger inside her. She kneaded his neck with her fingers and rubbed her thigh against his cock.

He rolled atop her. Her pelt abraded the underside of his prick with delicious friction. He pushed his butt up and back. Her legs parted. He lowered himself and slid smoothly into her.

Slowly, lovingly, he took her. Her fingers played up and down his back like a musician's over a keyboard. Her breasts were flattened against his powerful chest, and her hips stirred constantly in counterclockwise rotation around his prick.

Twilight faded into darkness. Gradually their embrace became more fervent, their mutual striving more vigorous. Deborah braced her slender feet against the brass rail at the foot of the bed and pushed hard with her legs, driving herself down hard upon him. His eyes bulged, and she laughed.

He pressed his own feet against the rail and started to fight fire with fire. He slid his hands under her rump. Her buttocks were firm and cool and muscular. He felt a rivulet of her lubricants run down over his fingers.

Suddenly she was clutching at him, smashing her hips into him. "Oh, God!" she cried. His hips took on a life of their own, pumping back and forth, and he felt himself explode within her as she crooned tunelessly to herself.

When he had spent himself he drew a deep sigh. He stroked her cheek. Her mouth was damp with their mingled saliva, and her hair had fallen in her face, giving her a mysterious, alluring look.

She touched his cheek timidly. "I love you," she said. "I don't know who or what you are. But I know I've never met a man like you."

He kissed her and held her tight. But he thought, *What can I tell this girl?*

But she did not press for an answer. In a while she began to importune with her fingers, and they loved again, hurriedly, before he had to make his way back to the wagon for the evening show.

For some reason, he had trouble looking his fellow operative in the eye.

Raider lay on his back with his hands behind his head, staring into the blackness and trying to think. *Ain't I in a pickle,* he said to himself. *And there's no way out.*

Henry Durán reckoned an old Jewish dry-goods merchant as his main opponent in Las Peñas. And Durán still bore the man's son David a grudge for blowing Jesus Saiz's head apart with his rifle. So the master Thief had hit on a scheme to neutralize the old man and bring the younger into his clutches at a single blow. A raiding party of Thieves was going to swoop down on Las Peñas tomorrow and kidnap the girl, in broad daylight.

And Raider was going to lead it.

It was a danger every Pink faced, of being forced to take part in crimes to avoid compromising a cover identity. It was hard to infiltrate a criminal band and *not* engage in criminal activities. The usual practice was to try to talk your "fellow" criminals out of whatever undertaking they had in mind for you. But there was no diverting Durán. Raider had a sneaking suspicion that his intention wasn't simply strategic. A certain gleam came into those yellow eyes whenever the name of Deborah Silver was mentioned.

Maybe Sallee ain't keeping him satisfied. Odd. He'd have thought it was the other way round, the way Sallee had been looking at him. Especially at dinner that night.

His impulse now was to cut stick and go. Two things kept him. First, neither he nor Doc were sticklers for doing things by the rule book—he recalled with a twinge that he was about a week in arrears filing the reports operatives were supposed to send daily to Chicago, at whatever risk. But it was beginning to look as if the only way the Forty Thieves were going to get busted was if Raider and his partner got their knuckles bloody busting it. That was good and well, but if they took any—well, extralegal—actions, they had to have a solid backing of evidence to justify their actions. Evidence that would stand up in court.

Raider could certainly testify to the murder of the hapless Clarence King. But who really cared about the death of a rummy, a failed gunslinger who hadn't measured up to the Thieves' exacting standards? What Raider lacked was solid proof that the death of Odelbert and the others was murder, and that Durán was responsible. And with everyone except Durán himself, Sancha, and Sallee angry and suspicious toward him because of Redeye's death, he hardly felt he could call attention to himself by asking everybody in sight if they'd helped rub out the Ballenkamp place. He needed to have somebody get talkative, and had no notion how to go about that.

Sallee. Maybe there was something there. He got the feeling she was none too happy about what was going on at the Castile.

His other reason for not bugging out was infinitely more basic. Durán had clamped the lid on tight tonight—lanterns hung all around the compound, the perimeter guards doubled—apparently in case Redeye's demise prompted anybody to try seeking employment elsewhere. Raider was far from a coward, but he had no desire whatsoever to wind up getting dragged into a bundle of bloody mush behind that bitch Sancha's stallion—and wouldn't *la dama* Durán just love that? More to the point, it wouldn't achieve much toward solving the case.

Showing too much reluctance to perform his assigned task would no doubt have the same result as an open attempt at desertion. Durán had rather expensive notions of how to encourage attention to duty, but damned if they didn't work.

From outside the door, a tiny sound. His Peacemaker appeared in his hand from its holster beneath the bed. He wouldn't put it past one of Durán's boys to try to settle Redeye's score with Raider in the dark of night, with a knife, say. He thought of the hot-eyed look Miguelito Díaz had given him that afternoon, and quietly drew back the hammer.

The latch lifted. The door opened. A female figure appeared in the gloom. Raider's guts knotted. *Sancha!* God, he couldn't touch her tonight—not after what he'd seen today. He found himself sweating cold, leveling the pistol with both hands at the dim shape. *No, you damn fool, you can't shoot her, that'll spoil everything!*

"Raider? Honey, it's me. Sallee."

The air streamed out of his lungs in a sigh of relief. He let in the trigger and laid the gun on the floor. Would he have shot Sancha Durán? Better not to have found out.

Sallee joined him on the bed. Her hair was still caught up on top of her head. She wore a floor-length robe of some silk that shone palely in the dim starlight that came in the window.

"What're you—" Her mouth clamped on his, shutting of the flow of words. Her tongue sought his as she squirmed against him, hands questing under the sheet for his prick. Her robe fell open, spilling her magnificent bare boobs against his chest. The nipples were ripe and taut cherries, firm against his chest.

He pushed her roughly away. "Have you gone crazy, woman?" he demanded. "What if Durán should come a-lookin' fer you?"

"He won't."

"Now how in tarnation kin you know *that?*"

She smiled. "Same way I know Miss Sancha won't be creepin' in on you, honey."

He stared at her. Durán and his *sister?* Jesus, these people were weird.

Sallee was on him again, with her tongue all over his. *What the hell?* he thought. He grabbed a handful of boob and kissed her back.

His dick didn't even need the skillful urging of her fingers to become rigid. The smell of her perfume, the soft clean feel of her skin, the rich creamy fullness of the tits squashed against him, all made him randy as a stallion. He pressed her to him, thrusting his cock at her.

She tore the sheet out from between them and swung a plump shapely leg across him. For a moment she posed there above him, with her tits hanging heavy above his eyes, the golden-furred patch of her bush poised tantalizing inches above the throbbing head of his cock. She reached up and unfastened her hair. It fell in a pallid star-silvered cascade about her shoulders.

She lowered herself, steering him into her with sure steady fingers. He bit his lip as her pussy enfolded him. A trickle of aromatic juice ran down the underside of his prick and across his balls.

He bucked his hips upward, half voluntarily. A squeal of pleasure burst from her lips. She put her palms on his flat belly and began to work her hips back and forth.

He reached up and grabbed both boobs. She raised her hands to his and crushed them against her snow-white breasts. They fucked like a house afire, the bed squeaking and groaning, Raider's cock working in and out of Sallee's cunt with a moist squelching sound. In a matter of seconds Raider felt his balls suddenly boil over. Sallee cried out and fell on top of him, mouth searching, begging. He felt her pussy tighten around him, milking the come from his spurting prick.

In time they relaxed. He lay there with the sweet warm weight of her atop him, with his hand under her robe, stroking the smooth silky curve of her back.

Something wet dripped onto his chest. He pushed his chin down and lifted Sallee's face with his free hand. "You're cryin'."

"I—I'm sorry." She dropped her eyes. The tears had streaked the makeup that ringed her blue eyes, making dark trails down her cheeks.

"Now, that ain't the way a lady normally acts when I'm done lovin' her," Raider said, trying to cheer her. "What's the matter."

"I'm scared."

He wrapped his arms around her and held her to him for long moments. Her body shook to sobs, long and wracking.

At last the shaking passed. "Rade," she said in a small voice. "Can I trust you?"

"You know it." He was holding his breath.

She pushed herself off to the side, biting her lip as his limp cock slid from her. "I want out," she whispered. "What I saw today—that was the last straw. I can't stomach it anymore. I can't *pretend* anymore." The tears began to flow freely again. "Henry promised he'd make me a princess. I'm nothin' but a concubine. And I wouldn't be a princess of this—this madhouse."

She propped herself up on one arm. "He has to be stopped. He's ruinin' this town. He's killed people and he's gonna keep on killin' unless somethin's *done*. And I can't take it anymore." She gazed at him, dry-eyed. "Now you can go runnin' and tell Henry, and he'll give you a big reward. And he'll give me to that monster of his. Abadón." She shuddered.

Raider lay on his back. He knitted his fingers behind his head and gazed upward. He could make out the bulky beams of the *vigas* now. "Sallee," he said softly, "you ever hear of the Pinkertons?"

He felt her quiver with the need to feel impossible hope. "Yes."

"I'm one of them. I got a partner here in town, workin' with me. Our job is to bust up the Forty Thieves and put Mr. Durán behind bars. But I need help."

She clutched his arm. "Anything!"

He turned his face toward her. "The Ballenkamp place. Do you know what happened there?"

"You bet I do!" Her voice was unexpectedly fierce. "That was the first thing that really soured me."

"What happened?"

"They killed them!"

Excitement coursed in Raider's veins. "Who? And how?" And in the deceptive peace of the mountain night, the half-naked blond woman began to recount the details of the slaughter at Hugo's Roadhouse.

CHAPTER ELEVEN

The riders swept down on Las Peñas that morning like a wind from hell.

Raider led five men down the trail from the Castile. With him were apple-cheeked David Apodaca, whom he'd met at Talley's; a skinny evil-looking Irish-Indian breed named Alfredo Chapman, who was nursing a sizable goose egg on the side of his head; a couple of *nativos,* Sammy Rodríguez and Martín Vigil; and Preacher Hanks, the Bible-toting stork of a killer who was one of Durán's lieutenants. Raider was in command of the group, but the presence of Hanks was a definite remedy against getting a swelled head. Durán obviously wanted someone he could be sure of trusting along on Raider's maiden mission. Someone who would without hesitation put a bullet through the new man if he stepped wrong.

They thundered through the wooded mountains, across streams, and along a narrow patch Raider had noticed on his first trip out to the ranch with poor Redeye, where a big cluster of rock jutted out over the trail on one side and the land fell away steeply to a forested gully on the other. Then they crested the final rise and came booming down on the defenseless town.

The Thieves gave tongue like hunting wolves as they burst in upon the town. It was just about mid-morning, and the streets were middling crowded. There was no attempt at disguise or sneaking or anything else. The residents of

Las Peñas were supposed to know who was visiting them this fine April morning, and why.

It was a Saturday, which meant that old Silver stayed home from the store with his daughter. Raider let the Thieves make their way to the street on which the old merchant lived. They did so at a gallop, scattering pedestrians before the flying hooves of their horses.

They reined in savagely, making their horses rear and whinny. "Away, you sinners!" Hanks shouted at the townsfolk who stood gaping along the side of the dirt street. "Don't you know the Devil finds work for idle hands?" He whipped out one of his pistols, an ancient Dragoon as long as his arm, and started flinging shots at random.

"*Hijo la,*" Sammy Rodríguez said with a grin. "I hope that crazy old *joto* don' throw one my way."

Without answering, Raider swung down off the bay. A hitching post stood near the corner of Silver's lot. He looped the reins through the verdigris-colored ring and ran up onto the porch. Chapman, Rodríguez, and Vigil followed close behind him, leaving Apodaca and Hanks behind, mounted, to watch their mounts and the extra horse they'd brought for Deborah and fend off rescue attempts, in the unlikely event any came.

Here goes nothin', Raider told himself. *Hope the old man don't keep a loaded scatter-gun next the door in a umbrella stand.* He raised a booted foot and kicked at the door. It refused to budge. "Shit!" he yelled, and threw his weight against it. The bolt ripped free of the jamb and the door swung inward.

"Who are you?" a female voice demanded from the top of the stairs, strident with defiance. "Leave this house at once!"

"That's her, *cuate,*" Rodríguez said. He bounded up the stairs toward the tall dark-haired young woman in the gray dress and jacket. She stared at him for a moment, then braced herself.

"My father is resting," she said. "I forbid you to disturb him."

"Shit, *chiquita*." Rodríguez grinned. "I don't aim to disturb him none." He grabbed her by the arm and tried to drag her down the stairs.

She didn't fight back. Neither did she go along. She was half a head taller than the Thief, and he was unable to budge her.

Raider just stood, unable to push forward and lay violent hands on this brave young woman. Hooting with laughter at their companion's distress, the other two raced up the stairs to join the fray.

"Here! What's going on here!" A frail old man appeared on the landing behind the woman. His hair and beard were gray, and a funny little knit wool skullcap clung to the back of his head. His black eyebrows bristled with outrage. "*Cossacks!* Unhand my daughter!"

He rushed forward and tried to pry Rodríguez's hands off the woman. Chapman snarled a curse and backhanded him. The old man toppled backwards, the skullcap flying from his head.

"Father!" the girl screamed. She hit at Chapman, staggering him. He howled, clutching the bump on his head.

Vigil slapped her hard. She screamed and clawed at his face. Rodríguez tugged abruptly on her other arm and she fell forward. Vigil flung her over his shoulder and laughingly carried her down the stairs.

Rodríguez followed. Chapman came last, still clutching his aching head. Raider stood transfixed as the Thieves bundled the struggling girl out the door into the street.

"My daughter, my daughter!" The old man was weeping now, crawling to the head of the stairs. "No, don't take her!"

Raider opened his mouth to reassure the old man. But Chapman reappeared in the doorway at that instant to cry, "Come on or we're leavin' you, straw boss or not." Raider turned his back on the old man's anguish and ran out the door.

And stepped into a scene from hell.

The street was full of riders—Thieves. Shots were being

fired, men were shouting, and women were screaming. A body lay in the street up the block, facedown in a scarlet pool of blood.

Raider vaulted into the saddle of his bay. "What the fuck's going on here?" he demanded.

Chapman gave him an ugly grin. "Hey, this little jaunt of ours is just a sideshow. We come to give Las Peñas a hoorawin' they'll not soon be forgettin'!"

They rode through the town, Chapman leading the sorrel to whose back the captive had been tied. The Thieves were everywhere, shooting out windows, riding their horses into buildings, walking out of shops with their arms piled full of plundered goods. Anyone who got in their way was ridden down. Raider saw half a dozen forms lying still in the street before reaching the plaza.

Mounted on a pinto the size of a Percheron, a vast sombrero bucking at his back, Marcosio Abadón thundered into the plaza from the north with McVie, Chacón, and several other riders at his back as Raider's group rode up from the south. A pretty teenaged *nativa* in white blouse and wide skirts stood on the boardwalk across from City Hall and the jail, staring in horror, her kid brother by her side. Whooping, Slowhand McVie set his mount racing for her. She stood transfixed, breaking and trying to run only when the big chestnut was almost on top of her. The towheaded gunfighter's horse pawed air as the girl darted under its hooves. He pivoted the animal, grabbed at her, missed.

Coming up behind, Abadón caught the girl's arm and swung her across the saddle as if she weighed nothing. She flailed and screamed hoarsely for help. He guffawed and tore open her blouse, baring the girl's round brown breasts.

Her brother screamed in Spanish, "Let her go!" and ran at Abadón. The giant pawed his sister's naked breasts as the boy pounded at him with impotent fists. Then the youth seized the man's thick arm in both hands and bit him on the wrist.

"*Hijo de la chingada!*" Abadón roared. His right hand

flashed to the machete slung across his back, brought it down in a glittering arc.

It split the boy's head like a cantaloupe.

Raider wanted to puke. More than that he wanted to slap leather and give the ogre a .44-40 ball in the guts, a bad wound that would leave him lingering in agony for days. But there was no way he could do it, no way. It wasn't fear for his own life that held his hand. It was his sense of duty—the knowledge that if he gave in to the hatred that raged inside him, he and Doc would have failed, that the reaving of the Forty Thieves would continue unchecked.

"Smite the Babylonians hip and thigh!" Preacher Hanks bellowed. His voice was surprisingly big to be coming out of that scrawny chest. Abadón shook blood drops off his machete and passed the hysterical girl to another rider. Trying not to see the horror taking place on every side of him, Raider took his party across the plaza at a gallop.

He'd been had. Mousetrapped. Durán was not yet completely satisfied as to his new lieutenant's loyalty. So he gave him a simple-seeming assignment—and then dropped him in the middle of an atrocity that would leave him and every other participant a marked man for life, with only the might of Henry Durán and his Forty Thieves standing between them and retribution.

Or maybe Durán didn't doubt him, but went ahead and dropped him into this foul kettle of massacre and rape to bind him more closely to his lord.

With a sense of relief Raider passed the northernmost houses of Las Peñas and rode for the Castile with his marauders strung out behind him.

Doc had just finished eating breakfast at Ramona's when he heard the commotion outside.

He hadn't felt like facing Judy over breakfast that morning, so he had wandered into town after awakening at nine. He'd been to Ramona's several times since arriving in Las Peñas. She had taken a shine to him, and referred to him as *mi guerito*, my blondie. He enjoyed chaffing with her. She was quite a beautiful woman, though a long way from young, and he might have considered trying to get to know her better if he didn't feel he already had more women on his hands than he was prepared to deal with.

"Seen any more of your tall, dark stranger?" he asked as she served him a meal of *carne adovada* and fried potatoes. Though he'd been careful not to be at the redhead's *taberna* at the same time as Raider, he'd heard enough talk to know his partner had caught Ramona's still-sharp eye. He had by this time heard all about the gunfight with Rynerson. It had concerned him, but he had held off acting, instinctively feeling that his partner knew what he was doing. His belief had been confirmed when he learned that Raider had been bailed out by none other than Henry Durán's sister, Sancha.

Ramona frowned. Her knuckles went white on the handle of the tin coffee pot with which she'd just refilled Doc's mug. "That *cabron*," she spat. "Don't talk to me of him."

Doc's eyebrows rose. "What happened?"

"He joined the Thieves." Her tone consigned him to the hottest depths of hell. She marched away. Doc admired the play of her buttocks beneath the denim of the jeans she wore under her apron. *Poor Rade. He's blown his chances there.*

He finished up the meal and started out the door. A cavalcade of armed men thundered by, the hooves of their horses barely missing him. He leapt back with a startled exclamation.

He never heard the shot, but suddenly a splinter of wood flew from the squared wooden upright by his head. He dodged back inside. Ramona and Jorge and the few other patrons stood at the window, peering out. "What's going on?" the tall redhead asked.

"It's the Thieves!" one of the patrons, a grizzled man in a shabby suit and tophat exclaimed. "They's shootin' up the town!"

"Shutter the windows and lock the doors!" Ramona ordered. Doc started out the door. "Where do you think you're going?" she rapped.

He was suddenly seized with a fever of urgency. "Got to get back to my wagon!"

"Not that way! They're like animals out there. You wouldn't make a block." Jorge had slammed the heavy door shut and turned the lock. The other customers were falling to with a will, closing the carved shutters on the windows.

For a moment Doc dithered. *She's right,* he thought. He raced for the back door, through the kitchen. Roberta cowered from him in terror as he ran by and burst into the alley behind the tavern.

Shouts and shots everywhere. He paused, took a breath and his bearings, and started off to the north, away from Central and the greatest commotion. Working cautiously, he made his way to the western fringe of town. Twice he passed people lying by the road. One was an old man who when rolled onto his back had a bluish-black indentation in his forehead, where a flying hoof had caught him. The other was a young man, moaning and clutching an arm shattered by a pistol ball. Doc hesitated. His every nerve cried out to get back to Judy at once. He wasn't really a doctor—but he was a healer, if only self-proclaimed, and he couldn't pass the youth by without doing what he could. He helped the man into a nearby house, where a stout gray-haired woman in an apron aided in staunching the bleeding. There wasn't much else he could do, so he gave the man one of the bottles of his Egyptian Cure that he always carried with him and ran out of the house.

He no sooner got to the edge of town and looked out across the fields to the Widow Whateley's than he knew he was too late.

Judy Holiday gave a good account of herself.

She was inside the AOA wagon tending to the various livestock Doc used in his act, including several white doves in cages and Sam, the boa constrictor, when she heard the tumult from town. *Shots*, she thought. Her blood chilled.

She moved to the rear of the wagon and looked out. She could see something going on in the town. *Doc*, she thought. *I hope he's all right*.

Moving methodically, she got the shotgun and the Winchester and laid them on crates of Egyptian Cure where they'd be ready to hand, with extra boxes of cartridges nearby—an optimistic touch, she knew. She picked up the rifle, jacked a shell into the chamber, and seated herself at the rear of the wagon to watch.

Minutes went by. The noise from Las Peñas was terrifying. The Thieves must be launching a major attack on the town—why, she did not know. She guessed that Doc Weatherbee's holdout Medicine Show would not be spared the tender attention of the marauders.

Then she saw them. Five men on horseback, spread out in a wide rank, coming from the village at a gallop. There was no mistaking their destination. She sat on the floor of the wagon, rested the rifle on the tailgate, and sighted on the center rider. *Steady, girl*, she told herself. She drew a deep breath, let it halfway out, squeezed the trigger.

The rifle slammed into her shoulder. Two hundred yards away her target slumped sideways off his horse. The animal screamed and bolted off across the path of the others.

Holiday smiled grimly. She worked the lever and raised the rifle again. She fired. A miss. The raiders were getting closer now. She fired again, more quickly, and felt a surge of triumph as a second rider reeled in his saddle and threw his hand to his arm.

From behind she heard a stealthy creak. *Someone's climbing in the front!* She started to spin.

A hand seized the shiny muzzle of the rifle.

She dropped the weapon at once. A man appeared at the arched front of the wagon canopy, dark against the pale blue sky and low-hanging fluffy clouds. He lunged. Holiday snatched up the shotgun and fired.

The muzzle blast seemed to deafen her. The man took the charge of buckshot full in the chest. It stopped him in mid-leap and threw him into a pile of luggage. He lay unmoving, making an unpleasant sucking-gurgling sound.

Strong arms seized her from behind. She swung the shotgun back over her shoulder one-handed. It glanced off her assailant's shoulder and the second barrel went, letting daylight through the canvas roof. Stunned by the blast so near his face, the man released her.

She bounded forward, caught up a covered wicker basket from atop a crate. The man was right behind, a chunky *nativo* in his thirties with black hair hanging in his eyes. "C'mere, baby," he said. "I won't hurt you none."

She threw the contents of the basket in his face. The man let out a surprised yell that was quickly cut off as Sam knotted around his neck in a spasm of mortal terror. Face blue, clawing at the snake that was crushing the life from him, the man staggered back and fell out over the tailgate.

She had the shotgun broken open and was stuffing shells into it when they swarmed her. One from the front of the wagon and two from the rear. She never had the chance even to snap the breech closed.

Kicking and scratching, she was hauled out into the daylight. The man on whom she'd dumped Sam was lying by the side with the frightened snake still clutching him in its coils. The man's boots were kicking feebly at the caliche, but no one paid him any mind.

Tall as a mountain atop his ponderous pinto, Marcosio Abadón watched impassively as Judy was hauled before him and forced to her knees. "The fucking bitch," one of her captors said in a Texas voice. "She like to put my eyes out. She finished poor Eduardo and Albert."

"Looks like Arellanes, too," someone else said, back out of her field of vision. "The snake, I think she like him too well." The others laughed.

"Let's tie her to the wagon and torch it," Texas said. Judy tried not to flinch.

"You may try if you are tired of living, Bennett, amigo,"

the giant said amiably. ''She has spirit, this one. She's mine.''

He looked her in the eye and smiled.

For the first time in her life, Judy Holiday screamed in fear.

CHAPTER TWELVE

"For God's sake, Mayor." The blond young man slammed a fist down on the polished maple top of the desk. "You've got to *do* something."

Mayor Stone had a square head, red face, and very white hair and side-whiskers. His face went a shade redder, making it clash with the pink shirt he was wearing under his black frock coat. "You can't take that tone with me, young fellow," he said sternly. From outside came the calls of workmen, the tinkle of broken glass being swept from the streets, and other sounds of the cleaning-up of the wreckage left by the morning's raid.

But the young man refused to be put off that way. "It's time somebody took that tone, Mayor Stone," he said, controlling his voice with obvious effort, "if it gets something done."

He was on the tall side, well-built, with very light blond hair and dark sideburns, a long handsome face, eyes gray behind wire-rimmed glasses. He wore beige trousers and vest. He held a wadded cotton rag to the right side of his head. It was pretty well soaked with blood.

Stone frowned. "Are you insinuating that this office is not doing everything in its power to relieve the situation?" he demanded. Doc had to give him credit for the conviction that pealed in his voice. The man was a born actor.

The young man laughed derisively. "Just what in hell's name are you doing? Mayor, six people are lying dead in

the street out there, five women have been kidnapped,
stores have been looted, property destroyed. Now tell me,
Your Honor, what *is* being done?''

"Now, Mr. Salem, you're in a responsible position in
this town too, don't forget—''

"Don't try to shift the blame!'' There was an edge of
hysteria to the outburst.

"—so I hope you will refrain from publishing irresponsi-
ble charges in the *Intelligencer*.''

The young man moaned, staggered back a step, and sat
down in one of the mayor's red-velvet upholstered chairs.
He'd been introduced to Doc a few minutes before as Lew
Salem, editor and publisher of Las Peñas's one and only
newspaper since the death of Francis Warren at the
roadhouse. He was one of the townspeople who had not
taken the Thieves' incursion lying down. He'd come out of
the newspaper office with pistol in hand, only to have one
of Durán's men crease his skull with a bullet, knocking
him cold. He had refused to take the time to get the wound
bandaged on awakening, and had come storming straight
to the mayor's office.

"My daughter,'' Benjamin Silver moaned. "Your Honor,
is there nothing you can *do?*''

Mayor Stone looked grave. "I am informed that Chief
Broward is pursuing a most vigorous investigation at this
very moment, sir.''

"*Investigation!*'' The word burst from Doc's lungs in an
explosion of disbelief. "What is there to investigate? The
Forty Thieves shot up the town. All that remains is to ride
out to the Castile and bring those responsible to account!''

The mayor's pale blue eyes blazed up. "Doctor, these
are serious allegations you are making. Henry Durán is a
well-respected member of this community. I am not prepared to sit here and listen to an outsider cast aspersions on
him.''

Doc sagged back in his chair. *Oh, Judy, Judy,* he
thought. *Oh, Deborah. Oh, shit.* He couldn't believe this
little man.

The crags of the mayor's face softened. ''The police are following up some very solid leads in this case, Doctor— gentlemen. For example, one of the raiders has been positively identified as a drifter who goes by the name of Raider, a tall, black-mustached scoundrel. A man, may I remind you, who was only recently incarcerated in this city for the unprovoked killing of one Richard Rynerson—an employee of this Henry Durán whom you are so eager to implicate, Doctor.''

''And who was bailed out by Sancha Durán.''

Another moan escaped Benjamin Silver's colorless lips. ''I know of this man—did he not invade my home and steal my daughter right before my poor old eyes? But he did not send those men to carry off Deborah or shoot up the town. It was Durán. Durán—may he burn!''

Doc recoiled at the force of the old man's exclamation, so different from his usual gentleness. The mayor sucked on his lips. ''I don't like to mention this, Benjamin,'' he said, ''but I can't help reminding you that at this moment your son David is a fugitive from justice—''

''*Justice!*'' It was torn from the old man as if by red-hot pincers.

''—which leads me to consider an alternative hypothesis. Is it possible that your son wished to be reunited with his sister? Or to hold her as a hostage, perhaps?'' He picked up a pen and scrawled on a pad beside his elbow. ''I must make a memorandum to suggest that possibility to the chief.''

Doc stood up, heartily sick of this charade. ''I can see Your Honor is a busy man.'' His words oozed sarcasm. ''I think I shall be about my business.''

Mayor Stone looked up and smiled. ''Thank you for your consideration, Doctor. And thank you, gentlemen, for taking the time to share with me—''

The sudden silence outside the open window of the second-story office drew their attention like a magnet. Cutting across the stillness came the mathematically precise slow-march of a horse's shod hooves walking up the street outside. Doc went to the window. Lew Salem was immediately at his side.

It was a single rider on a high-stepping sorrel with four white stockings. The man wore a white pin-striped shirt, brown vest, trousers, and hat, with a green scarf knotted around his neck. The face beneath the hat brim was dark-skinned, clean-shaven, leanly handsome. "*Chacón!*" Salem spit the name out like poison.

Doc recognized him too, and stilled the urge to reach into his coat for his short-barreled Lightning. Killing him would help neither Judy nor Deborah.

The Thief took a cigarette from his mouth with a gloved hand. "*Ódale,* Mayor. You in there?"

Some of the flush was missing from the mayor's face as he came around the desk to the window. His chair was placed on some sort of built-up platform to make him look taller when he sat behind his desk; on his legs he was scarcely five feet tall. "I'm here," he said in a carrying voice.

"Somebody told me that the old Jew is up there too."

Painfully Silver hobbled to the window. "I'm here. What do you want?"

"Not much, old man. Mr. Durán wants for you to stop stirring people up against him."

The old man swallowed heavily, but said nothing. "And he wants David," the gunman said.

"*No!*" The old man sank to his knees.

Chacón shrugged. "Think about it, old man," he said casually. "Take a day—take two; Señor Durán is a generous man." He tossed the cigarette away and took another from his vest pocket. "Do what you're told, or you'll get your little girl back—in pieces. Maybe one of those long legs of hers first, perhaps." He scratched a match on his saddle horn and lit up.

"Animal," Lew Salem said.

"You had an accident today that scrambled your brains, Mr. Salem," Chacón said lightly. "So I'll forget you said that. *Buenos dias.*'' He turned the sorrel's head and nudged it into a lazy walk.

"Wait!" Doc called. "What about—what about Madame Teresa? My assistant.''

Chacón shrugged. "Abadón got her," he said, as if he were saying *plague took her*. "Maybe he'll let you have her back when he's done with her.'' He took the cigarette from his mouth and studied it. "Of course, she might not be much use to you. *Quién sabe?*'' He sent the sorrel trotting off, raising little swirls of dust with its hooves.

The sun sank into the trees on the ridge to the west of the villa. Raider sat on his bed in his room with his knees drawn up under his chin, toying with the whiskey bottle in his hands. To him it looked as if the fat orange orb of the sun was being scooped up by a toothy lower jaw. He was uncomfortable with his imagination, so he took another swallow of the whiskey, hoping to anesthetize it.

What a day. What a hell of a day. The things he'd seen in town! Raider was not a soft man, and he'd seen more than his share of troubles. But the things he'd witnessed in Las Peñas today touched something in the heart of him. He felt no guilt; he'd been constrained by his duty, which right now amounted to making sure no repetition of today's events was possible. There had been nothing he could do.

But the look in that pretty Jewish girl's eyes—as if he were lower than dirt. He'd earned the look, as far as she knew. *But she's a hostage,* he told himself. *They ain't gonna hurt her none.*

Was it the booze, or was the self-reassurance beginning to ring flat in his ears?

Screams came dimly to his ears. *Sounds like they're inside, this time.* He shuddered and drew deeply from his whiskey.

That had been the worst, he decided. Watching what they did to those three young women they'd dragged with them out of Las Peñas. The one they'd bent naked over a hitch rack with her wrists tied to her ankles and took turns with. The little *nativa* whose brother Abadón had hacked down, on her knees in front of Preacher Hanks taking his skinny dick in her mouth while he whipped her with a crop, shouting, "Take that, you whore of Babylon! Repent, repent, you greasy brown bitch!" The plump girl with the round face and the wiry red hair, incredibly fair-skinned, they swarmed all over, three of them forcing themselves on her at a time.

They'd laughed at a look of disgust he hadn't been able to hide. "Shit, man," Alfredo Chapman laughed. "You think this is bad, you should see what Abadón does to his. He likes to get 'em stuck on that big dick of his and fuck 'em until they really start to likin' it." He chuckled, "And they do, they do."

"What happens then?" Raider couldn't help asking.

"Why, he strangles 'em." The half-breed turned away, laughing. "Hey, Toby, Ygnacio, what say we hunt up some red ants and see if they'll put some sparkle back in that little redhead?"

Raider shook his head. He wondered if Abadón had brought a victim back today. He hadn't seen the giant since the awful scene at the plaza.

Shit! If there was something he could *do*. But he had to wait, at least until he could find a way to smuggle Sallee and himself away from the Castile. Then they'd have the evidence to move. Busting this ring was a job he was going to purely relish.

A knock at the door. He set the whiskey bottle down and pulled out his .44. No telling who might have been celebrating hard enough to want to go talk with the new boy about pore ol' Redeye. "Who is it?"

"Slowhand."

The voice fit. And Raider knew the towheaded gunslinger never had much use for King. Raider stood up, stuck the pistol in his pants, and padded barefoot to the door.

McVie was leaning against the frame. "Mr. D. wants you," he said in his slow lazy way. "Down in the basement."

"Basement? Din't know there was one."

The youth grinned as if at a private joke. "Don't normally have 'em, hereabouts. Too damn tough to dig 'em in the caliche. But, shit, this old house got lots of surprises."

Raider sat on the bed and pulled on his boots, buckled on his gunbelt, and stuck the pistol in its holster. Slowhand leaned in the doorway and watched with a half smile. "Let's go," Raider said.

The stairs to the basement were way at the back of the house, next to the pantry. McVie opened a door and nodded Raider through. To his surprise the air that washed over his face was hot, not cool, as air from belowground generally was. "Phew," he said. "What's that stink? They been branding cattle down there?"

McVie shrugged. Raider walked down the stairs. Red brick tiles like those in the foyer lined the side of the stairway. No mere hole in the dirt, this basement. He could see it was brightly lit with the yellow-white glare of kerosene lamps. He reached the tiled floor at the bottom of the stairs and turned.

And stopped dead.

A nude woman hung by her wrists from chains looped over a big hook in the ceiling. Blond hair, lank with sweat, hung in her face. Her fair, fair skin was crisscrossed with welts and weals.

Sancha Durán stood nearby, looking very prim in her riding habit. She held a riding crop flexed between her black-gloved hands. "It seems this brainless blond creature was caught rummaging though Henry's effects," she purred.

Raider felt the hard muzzle of a gun pressing into his kidneys, heard the click as McVie pulled back the hammer. "Shit," he said.

Sallee raised her head. Her face was bruised. "The diamonds," she whispered through cracked lips. "I didn't want to leave without my diamonds. Sorry, Rade."

Sancha reached to a small hearth in the wall at her side and took an iron rod from a bed of coals. The tip glowed cherry-pink. She looked at it a moment, then pressed it to the skin of Sallee's left buttock. Sallee shrieked.

Sancha smiled. "She sings nicely, doesn't she? You wouldn't believe the song she sang for me, Raider, *querido*. Perhaps you'll sing for us too—Mr. Pinkerton Detective."

"I'll see you fry first," he gritted.

Sancha laughed. "Oh no. Sallee perhaps. Maybe you as well—certain select parts of you, *comprende?*" She jerked her head. "Strip him and hang him up."

Hands grabbed him from behind. He tensed to fight back, willing to take a desperate risk for the slimmest chance of survival—or quick death. Sancha smiled and held the still-glowing iron near the nipple of Sallee's breast. The blonde whimpered and tried to flinch away. "Make it easy on her, my love."

Recalling the way those full, snowy breasts had felt pressed to either side of his cock the night before, Raider stood glowering and allowed Slowhand and the Thieves who had come into the cellar behind him pull off his shirt and gunbelt and clamp his wrists in manacles chained to staples set high in the wall across from the hearth. The smooth red tile felt cool against his bare chest and belly.

"You know Cesario Blea, don't you?" came Sancha's voice, sweet and insinuating. Raider craned his neck. The *nativo* stood there, shirtless, looking even more muscle-bound than before. He held a black bullwhip in his hand. "He is a very strong man. Perhaps as strong as that animal Abadón." She set the cooling iron back among the embers. "Now we shall see how strong you are. Cesario."

The whip whistled through air. Raider braced himself for the bite of it. The impact jolted him like a hammerblow. Pain seared in a transverse slash across his back. He closed his eyes.

He was ready for the second cut, but he was still barely able to keep from crying out. At the last fraction of a second he clamped his teeth on his lower lip. *Won't cry out.*

The third stroke was the worst pain imaginable.
The fourth stroke was worse.

"Judy." A voice was calling her name from a million miles away. "Operative Holiday—wake up! You must wake up!"

She shifted. Pain lanced up through her belly. *God, what happened?*

"Judy, please wake up. Can you hear me?"

The voice was feminine. She wished it would go away. It was nagging at her, calling back to pain and the memory of—

Suddenly she was fully awake. And she knew what had happened to her.

She gave a huge shuddering sigh. "Judy! Are you all right?" the voice asked, vibrating with concern.

She made herself nod. "Just—just a moment," she said. She had to steel herself to open her eyes.

She remembered it all—the fight at the wagon, the nightmare ride in the procession of jeering Thieves to the Castile—and then, in that little room, with Abadón leering down at her as he stripped the shirt from his massive chest.

And I swooned like a schoolgirl. No sooner had she had the thought than she knew it was untrue. She hadn't fainted—not then. Only later, when her body and mind wouldn't take any more.

So it had happened. The special risk that a female Pinkerton ran that her male counterpart didn't. The Fate Worse than Death. Almost. She smiled. She still didn't know a fate worse than death. Close, but not quite.

She took stock of herself. The female presence in the room, still unseen, took her hand and held it. *I'm still the same woman I was before—before—*

But that wasn't true. Now she wanted to see someone die. Slowly.

God, he was huge. I didn't know men could be like that, more like a horse than a man. Christ, the pain! As if I was full of broken glass.

She put the recollections from her and opened her eyes. A lovely face looked down at hers, slanted eyes filled with concern. "Deborah," she whispered. She screwed her eyes shut. "Dear God, not you *too*."

She made herself sit up. "Are you sure you should do that?" Deborah asked.

Judy nodded. "I have to do it sooner or later. Might as well do it now." She swung her legs over the side of the low bed. "Is there water?"

They were in a small room with a wood floor, lit by a lantern hanging from a hook. The door looked heavy. There was a little barred grate set into it at eye level. *How convenient*, Holiday thought. *Durán has one wing of his home set up as a prison*.

Deborah rose from her side and walked over to a rude wood table, a few rough-hewn blocks cobbled together, on which stood a cracked white pitcher. She gave it to the agent, who drank greedily from the mouth.

Judy was naked but for an itchy wool blanket. Her clothes hadn't survived, she recalled. The taller woman was dressed in a long white robe and seemed to have nothing beneath. She sat down next to the agent.

"Durán's men. They came for me today. It was just my father and me—we didn't have a chance." She moistened her lips with her tongue. "I heard . . . I heard you fought them."

"Much good it did me," Judy said. "No. I don't mean that. I'm glad I fought. I killed three."

Deborah looked at her hand, lying in her lap like helpless bird. "I always thought it was wrong to kill, to *want* to kill. Now I do not know."

Judy touched her shoulder. *Don't think about the pain, girl*. "Have they—harmed you?"

Deborah shook her head. "No. It was very strange. I was locked in a room for a time by myself. Then I was taken to a bedroom, upstairs. The woman was there, the black-haired one. Sancha. She was wearing a black robe.

She looked very beautiful, and terrible at the same time, does that make sense?'' Judy nodded.

''She told me to undress. I did. She looked at me for a long time, then sat on the bed and told me to sit beside her. I did that too. I didn't know what else to do.

''She started to—to fondle me. My breasts, my stomach. 'You're very beautiful,' she said. 'The most beautiful child I've ever seen.' She let her robe fall open. She was naked underneath. She wanted me to . . . to touch her. I wouldn't. She had a short riding whip, and hit me with it. I tried to get away, but she grabbed my arm. She had the strongest grip of anyone I've ever known.

''I don't know what would have happened, but just then the door flew open. Mr. Durán stood there. He looked at his sister, and his eyes lit up like . . . like two lanterns. I think he was mad enough to kill her.

'' 'She's mine, damn you,' he shouted. She stood up and faced him. She didn't try to close her robe.

'' 'I want her. I claim her,' she said.

''He called her a bitch. She laughed at him. He started to whine. 'But I won't have Sallee now,' he said. 'I want her.'

''Sancha said something very strange then. 'You have me, my brother.' She went up to him and began stroking his neck. He called to his men and they brought me in here. They brought you in a while later—a half-hour or so ago.''

Judy shook her head. The rumors she had heard in town, and what Doc had learned and relayed to her, indicated there was a very strange ménage indeed here at the Castile. She hadn't realized how strange it was.

''We have to get you out of here.'' Pain stabbed through her belly. ''And me too.'' *Maybe it wasn't a fate worse than death,* she thought, *but I'd die before I'd go through it again.* ''I wonder if there's some way to get word to Raider.''

The girl frowned. ''Raider—the tall man, dark, with the

mustache?'' Judy nodded. ''But he was the one—he led the party that kidnapped me.''

''Damn.'' She actually felt a pang of pity for him. This was turning out to be an ugly assignment all around. ''He was supposed to be infiltrating Durán's gang,'' she explained. ''He must have had to do it, to prove his loyalty.''

Deborah nodded. ''I understand.'' To her own surprise Judy thought she did. She was an intelligent young woman, and seemed quite resilient. ''But—''

''What? What's the matter?''

''He's in the room across the hall. They brought him in right after you.''

''Yes?''

''He was unconscious.'' She choked on sudden tears. ''He'd been whipped till his back was in tatters!''

CHAPTER THIRTEEN

"Guard! Guard! Oh hurry, hurry, she's dying!" Judy Holiday's voice pealed through the grate in a tocsin of panic.

Boots clumped down the corridor outside, walking fast, not running. A snarling face was pressed to the grille. "What the fuck is the noise about? If it ain't important, you're gonna wish Abadón had finished you off, *gringa*."

Judy stood back. "It's her. She's started to throw up blood. It's terrible! Get a doctor, quick!"

The turnkey stared in at Deborah Silver. The girl was curled into a knot on the bed. Her chin was red with blood, and the blanket was dark and sodden.

"*Hi jo la!*" the guard exclaimed. He knew what the Jewess meant to Henry Durán, or part of it, at least. He knew for sure what would happen to him if he let anything happen to *her*. "Just a minute. Lemme see what's the matter."

He fumbled with a key ring. A moment later there was a scraping in the lock and the door swung open. The man had wits enough to close and lock the door behind him before rushing over to bend over the stricken hostage.

"Girl? *Judía?* Are you all right?"

She reached out and grabbed his wrists imploringly.

And Judy hit him in the head with the pitcher.

"*Ai, chinga!*" he shouted as the porcelain vessel shattered. He fell across Deborah, blood spurting from his cut head

159

to join that already liberally smeared about—Judy's on the blanket, and Deborah's from a cut she'd given herself on the lip with one fingernail. He tried to rise. Judy flung herself on his back and dragged him to the floor.

"Get his gun!" Deborah hissed.

The guard was still battling. Judy grabbed his head in both hands and cracked it against the floor, once, twice, three times. A curious shudder passed through the man's body. Then he was still. Very still.

Deborah stared at him, eyes round, cheeks pale. Judy hurriedly relieved him of his key ring and sidearm. As an afterthought she unbuckled his gunbelt and strapped it around her narrow waist, as much to keep her blanket in place as for the reloads. "Let's go."

"But—you killed him."

"Damned right. Come on. Someone might have heard."

She peered cautiously out the door. There was no one else in the corridor. She stole up to the other door and pressed her lips to the grate.

"Raider," she hissed. Silence. "*Raider.*"

Nothing. She made her fingers move purposefully as she sorted through the keys on the ring, trying one after the other. She sensed Deborah behind her, thanked God the girl knew enough not to hover, for all that her nerves must be screaming *hurry up!*

At last a key turned in the lock. She practically fell through the door. Raider lay on his belly on a bed like the one in the room just vacated, one forearm cradling his head, the other hanging limply to the floor. His back—

You can't get sick now, girl. She made her eyes overlook the bloody ruin and went to kneel by the bed.

She felt his wrist. "Still got a pulse. Raider, Raider— wake up, you sonovabitch!"

He shuddered. His head lolled to the side. One brown eye opened. "Judy Holiday," he whispered. "Where'd a girl like you learn to cuss like that?"

"Cut the gallant horsecrap," she snapped. "Can you walk?"

He closed his eyes. She thought he'd lapsed into oblivion again and shook him. "Hey, leave off, girl. I'm jest tryin' to tell if my innards'll come loose if'n I stirs off this bed."

The two women got him to his feet. With an arm around each of their necks he could sort of stagger. "You gals just clear the hell on out of here," he said blearily. "You won't get far with me to hold you back."

"The Thieves are all blind drunk," Judy whispered. "Nobody's going to see us—but keep your damned voice down anyway!"

They reached the end of the corridor. It gave into a hall running from the front of the house to the back, to the kitchen. After confirming that the coast was clear, as far as they could see or hear, they turned right, toward the rear.

The kitchen was deserted as they crept past the door. Raider was getting stronger, at least to the point he could walk almost unaided. They passed a sturdy door. From the other side came a muffled scream that set Judy's teeth on edge. "Jesus," Raider said.

The women looked at him. There was nothing to be done for Sallee now. "Let's move."

Out into the blackness of the night. A few torches showed on the wall, but no sentries were in sight. Tonight celebrating held a lot higher priority than guard duty. Besides, who was there to guard against, with the damned townies whipped like curs?

They stole across the rear of the courtyard. Loud snoring sounds emerged from the stables. The horses penned in the corral outside the high adobe wall snorted and stamped nervously, sensing something was amiss.

Judy peered into the stable. A lantern hung from a post. A single guard dozed with his back against the wall and a rifle by his side. She walked in very quietly, smacked him upside the head with the pistol butt, and he slept more soundly.

The immense black stallion bobbed his head and rolled his eyes, muttering uneasily low in his throat. "Easy, boy, easy. Come on, you two, help me get these horses out of here!''

There were three horses in the stables—the black, Durán's buckskin mare, and a spotted gray gelding, the haciendado's second-favorite mount. "None of us is gonna ride that big black bastard," Raider muttered. "We'll have to get another from the corral."

Halters with leads hung from pegs. The tackhouse next door was locked, with no way to get in without making noise. Judy and Deborah fixed halters on the gray and the buckskin and led them out to the small side gate. It was barred on the inside. Raider lifted it, gently, gently.

Pain spasmed through his shoulders as he lifted the bar clear of the brackets. He dropped the heavy plank to the ground, where it rang like a bell.

"Hey!" a voice cried from the corner of the wall. "What's going on there?"

Raider heaved against the gate with his shoulder, grinding dust and filth into his open wounds. "Let's go!" he shouted as confused cries rang from different parts of the compound.

Deborah darted back into the stable. "Fool woman," Raider cursed. "Where'd she go?" The angry trumpet of Sancha's black stallion answered him. A heartbeat later the huge horse burst from the stable and thundered out of the gate like a landslide, almost bowling over the humans and the other two horses.

"Mount up behind me," Judy yelled to Deborah. A shot cracked from the wall. The muzzle-flame stabbed outwards, into the night. Apparently the shooter thought the villa was under attack from without.

Lithely Deborah climbed over the peeled-log fence of the corral. "You two go on," she said. "I'll catch up with you."

"But—" Judy began.

Another shot. This bullet moaned overhead. "*Go!* I'll scatter the horses so they can't follow." Even as she spoke the tall young woman was hauling open the gate, spilling frightened horses in a flood into the darkened valley.

"We cain't leave you," Raider protested. He was having trouble staying on board the gray, clinging to the mane with one hand like the greenest of greenhorns. Lights were coming on inside the house now, and voices were calling questions and challenges.

"If they catch me you can come back for me—only *ride!*" Deborah screamed. Judy and Raider turned their purloined horses' heads and booted their flanks.

They were off, barreling across the darkened meadowland with the wind cool and sweet in their faces. It would have been exhilarating, had the two Pinkertons not been half dead from abuse and riding for their lives. Raider glanced over his shoulder. The compound was filling up with light now. Deborah still stood in the corral, shooing the last of the panicked horses on out into the darkness. As he watched, she grabbed the last straggler's mane and hauled herself aboard.

Instantly she was surrounded by men. She tried to charge through them, but one waved a torch in the horse's face. It spooked and threw her to the ground.

"Oh, Christ," Raider moaned.

Judy glanced back. "Ride!" she yelled. It was a pain-racked sob.

They rode.

"I don't understand," David Silver said. "That man upstairs kidnapped my sister. Now you tell me he had to do it. *Why* did he have to deliver her to those monsters? *Why?*"

For what seemed the tenth time today Doc explained once again the nature of Raider's assignment and what it entailed. "His only chance—the only chance for you and all your fellow townspeople—was to go along until he had the opportunity to act. He didn't know why Sancha and Durán wanted her—he only thought she'd be a hostage, and therefore safe. *He didn't know.*"

"And my sister is still a captive!" He jumped to his feet and paced a tight switchback on the flowered carpet of his father's sitting room.

Judy Holiday leaned forward. She was sitting next to Doc on the sofa, wearing a fresh blouse and skirt, and except for a few bruises on her face and the dark circles around her eyes looked as if nothing had happened. "Your sister allowed herself to be recaptured so that Raider and I would be sure of escaping," she said. Her voice was taut from the effort of holding in the pain she felt, physical and mental. "Don't you think we should waste less time on recriminations and try to figure out the best way to save her?"

David paced two more circuits, then sat down abruptly on a chair and threw up his hands. "We—yeah. You're right."

It was overcast outside, a gray and cheerless morning. As it happened, Doc hadn't had to stumble around the woods in the dark hoping to run across David Silver. He'd stumbled across him instead at the Las Peñas *Intelligencer*, where he'd gone to haul Lew Salem out of his bed in the apartment above the office to ask if he knew where Silver could be found. Having heard of his sister's kidnapping and the Thieves' ultimatum, he had come into town for a council of war with his co-conspirators.

All four of them.

They heard a tentative footstep at the top of the stairs and looked up to see Benjamin Silver descending. His back was bent by his worries, and his face was ashen.

"I have been speaking to your Mr. Raider," he said, his voice so soft as to be barely audible. "It is incredible that I should converse with the man who abducted my daughter. More so that I should feel sorry for him, as he lies injured in the poor child's bed." He shook his head. "I should have learned long ago to be surprised by nothing in this life."

"How is he?" Holiday asked.

Silver shrugged. "Better than can be expected, I think.

If he drinks any more of the Doctor's, ah, *Cure*, I fear for his health.''

"I think he needs it right now, Mr. Silver," Doc said.

"What? Oh. I beg your pardon. My mind was wandering."

You were thinking, "Why couldn't Deborah have escaped, and one of these strangers been left behind," Doc knew. *And who can blame you?*

Benjamin Silver sat down on a chair across from David's. "I would give up my attempts to bring Durán to justice," he said. "I could even—may God forgive me—agree to return the 'Pinkerton spy' to the Forty Thieves, as they demanded in their new ultimatum this morning. But I cannot ask you to surrender yourself, David. Not after what I saw yesterday. You are right; the law in the territory is rotten right through, and we can expect nothing of it."

David leapt to his feet, ran to the old man's side, and hugged him. "At last! At last you're ready to fight them, Father!"

But the old man pushed him away. "To fight, never." He took his son by the shoulders and made the younger man face him. "Listen to me. What have you to fight with? Four friends, two strangers—one of whom can barely move, should not move for at least a week—and a girl. Are they enough to take on the Forty Thieves?"

"All I know is, we have to *try*." There were tears in David's eyes.

His father still shook his head. "If you try, all will be lost."

David tore away. "Do you never learn? The only choices are to give in—or fight."

"Your father is right, in that we don't have much to fight with," Judy said.

He waved a hand at her. "You've no need to worry. You're not involved in this part."

"Mr. Silver, I *am* involved," she said in a low, tense voice. "Every bit as much as you are."

He sat down again. "I'm sorry. I should think before I speak. Or act." He grinned disarmingly.

His father stood. He came to David and kissed him on the forehead. "If only you'd thought of that twenty years ago." He turned and tottered into the kitchen.

David shook his head. "Poor Papa. Now look—we can get the townspeople behind us, I know we can."

"If they aren't behind you now," Doc said, "I don't see how. After what happened yesterday."

"They just need direction. Someone to show them the way."

"You? David, do you think Broward will hesitate a moment before throwing you in a cell if you try to drum up support?" Doc asked.

The young man rubbed his face. "I don't know. Anything's better than just bowing our heads and waiting for the ax. Isn't it?"

Judy looked at him, then at Doc. "I don't care how bad the odds are, Doctor," she said. "I'm willing to take the chance, to pull down Durán and his big white house. And I think Raider feels the same way."

"And you think you're going to take part in this?" David asked incredulously.

"Yes." Her tone didn't invite disagreement.

They sat for a while in silence. "Isn't your father taking rather a long time to get a glass of water?" Judy asked.

David sprang to his feet as though electrified. "My God!" he cried, and raced back into the kitchen. They heard him curse, and then the back door was flung open and they heard running steps.

Doc and Judy raced one another for the kitchen. The back door stood open to the alley. Through it Doc saw that one of the two stall doors in the little outbuilding stood open, and that the venerable chestnut was gone.

Judy picked up a scrap of paper off the stove. She read it and sagged back. "Dear God."

"What?" She held the paper out to him.

Maybe they will accept my sacrifice, read the shaky handwriting. *May God keep you always, my son.*

The sun was past the zenith, occasionally visible through sullen clouds, when David Silver laid his father's body on the boardwalk in front of City Hall. He straightened and stood a moment, breathing heavily from the effort of carrying the old man half a mile.

"Listen to me!" he shouted at Mayor Stone's window. His voice filled the windswept emptiness of the plaza. "My father went out to give himself up to your precious Durán. He wanted to spare any further bloodshed. They"—his voice cracked—"they didn't let him get twenty feet into the woods. They shot him, and they left him there to die like a dog."

He pointed to the still, gray form. "Here lies the last Silver to die like a dog—a kind, gentle old man who only wanted to save his fellow men from harm. This Silver will die like a man. If any of you—Broward, Stone—if you think you can lock me up, then come out and try. Or kill me where I stand. Because when I leave this spot I'm going into the mountains, and I'm going to pull the Castile down around Henry Durán's goddamned ears!"

He stood staring up at the window. It stared blankly back. He waited for the door of the neighboring police station to open, but it stayed shut. Maybe no one was home.

Silence stretched, and the never-ending whistle of the wind blew through it. Across the plaza the door of Robertson's Hardware opened and Luke Robertson emerged. He stood a moment, squinting up through his glasses at the sky as if in hopes of catching a glimpse of the sun. Then he hitched his gunbelt unfamiliarly up around his middle-aged spread and walked across the plaza, between the almost-naked cottonwoods, to stand at David Silver's side. Other doors opened; other men came out. None spoke. They all drifted, as though by accident, to stand huddled around the grieving young man, until there were more than twenty.

For a minute he stood as if unaware of them. Then he stooped and picked up his father once again. Sensing that this burden he must bear himself, no one offered to help. But when he started walking toward his father's house they all followed. Still without a word.

"Yep." Raider nodded sagely and took a swig from his bottle of Doctor Weatherbee's Patented Egyptian Cure. "I got it all worked out." He squinted at the bottle. His eyes had taken on a rather owlish appearance. He was sitting up in the bed of Deborah Silver's room, holding forth to the four people crammed into it. His chest was completely wrapped in white bandages. Red spots had begun to appear on the back where blood was soaking through. "Say, this here thing's empty. C'n you rustle me up another?"

David Silver looked at his friend Lew Salem. Salem shrugged. "Are you sure you should—" Judy Holiday began.

Doc fished another bottle from his coat pocket, started to toss it over, then thought better of it and handed it to his partner. "Here."

Raider accepted it, tried to twist out the cork, finally settled on prying it out with his teeth. "Damned if I ever thought I'd see the use of this swill," he remarked, and took a slug.

He blinked, shook his head, and wiped his mouth with the back of his hand. "Now, you understand everybody who's in on the town part of this has to wear a mask, 'cause we're gonna have to bend the laws some." Four heads nodded. He nodded with them for a moment, then caught himself. "Good. And you got the men all picked out to raid the Castile, David?" The young man nodded. His face was impassive. The others all knew how keen his grief was, but the prospect of action eased his pain far better than Doc's laudanum could have.

"Well, you-all can explain the details to the other group leaders you got picked out. Meantime, I needs three things."

"What are they?" Doc asked, a trifle sharply. He hated when Raider played drunken-coy.

"First, a good explosives man. Second, a crate or two of dynamite."

David and Lew traded glances. "Geordie McCassick," Lew said. "He's an old hard-rock miner. He'll do."

"We can get those," David affirmed. "What else do you need."

Raider held up the empty bottle. "Another one of these li'l rascals."

CHAPTER THIRTEEN

For a night and a day no Thieves had come to Las Peñas.
They had been too busy celebrating the humbling of the
town. The sun had just about set, without once showing its
face without a veiling of cloud, on the day of Benjamin
Silver's death when they started filtering in. Eight of them
turned up in the town's three watering holes.

At six-thirty the front door of the police station opened.
Scrawny Charlie, the desk man, glanced up from his soli-
taire game and froze in the act of turning up a down card
so he could peek at it. "Just stay nice and quiet," said a
man's voice. It was muffled, as far as Charlie could see,
by a bandanna tied over its owner's face. But he wasn't
too sure, because he found it hard to concentrate on much
beyond the yawning twin muzzles of the shotgun pointed
toward his face.

Broward was examining the contents of an important
file—marked "W" for whiskey—with two of his officers
when the masked intruders walked in. In short order the
chief, Charlie, Jailer Adams, and the other two were safely
locked away in one of their own cells.

"You'll never get away with this!" Broward bellowed as
the barred door clanged shut.

"Of course we will," said the man with the shotgun.
He was of medium height, stocky, and surprisingly well
dressed for a desperado. The bangs that showed beneath
the rim of his derby were yellow, and the eyes that danced

above his mask were blue. He led his three masked followers out the front, not neglecting to troll up the chief's file—which was half full yet—and mounted a slightly disgruntled looking mule while the others swung onto horseback. He aimed the mule's nose north and rode.

Bennett Wix sat back in the green pastel-painted chair with his back propped against Ramona's wall and watched the innkeeper's every move intensely as she took orders from her other customers. There weren't many tonight, and they were all keeping well clear of the four Thieves over by the front window.

"Hey, Ramona, honey, business don't look too good tonight," he called.

She walked tiredly around behind the bar and collapsed onto her elbows. "I'll get by, esé."

He pulled a face full of feigned concern. "Tell you what. I think it's about time you come out to the Castile with me. Change of scenery'll do you good."

She shook her head. "I don't think so, Benito."

Sammy Rodríguez leaned back and pulled at the end of his mustache. "Could be you got no choice, querida."

Wix grinned through his sandy mustache. One of his upper front teeth was prominently chipped, thanks to Doc having clipped him under the jaw with his walking stick. "Don't worry, darlin'. You don't even have to wait till you get out to the ranch. You can enjoy my company right here in this cosy little tavern of yours." He looked at his companions. They grinned, avid for this new game.

Ramona made a face. She thumped the bottle she had been polishing on the bar three times.

Four masked men raced out from the kitchen. Even taken by surprise Wix was no slouch. He started to rise, hand on the butt of his gun. One of the masked men stepped behind the bar, leaned an elbow on it, and fired a blast from a shotgun. The charge blew Wix's head all over the wall that Ramona and Roberta had just finished scraping Dick Rynerson off of.

Sammy's Colt cleared leather. Before he could fire, a volley crashed from the carbine and two pistols held by the other intruders. He half spun, put his hand against the wall, gave a shuddering sob, and sank to the floor, leaving bright trails of blood on the whitewash.

"Hands up!" the shotgunner rapped in Spanish. The two Mexicans raised their hands.

"Don't kill us," one said.

"Clean up the mess your friends made," Ramona told them, "and I may try to talk them out of it."

Within ten minutes all eight Thieves in Las Peñas were accounted for: four dead and three captured, one of the latter wounded. The townsfolk's only casualty was Eloy Martínez's older son, Xavier, shot in the leg by Martín Vigil, who had helped kidnap Deborah Silver. Vigil himself fetched up dead a moment later, riddled from three different directions.

That left the eighth Thief. His shoulder gouged painfully by a bullet, David Apodaca managed to dodge out the back door of Talley's while his pal Vigil was being perforated, grab his horse, and ride like the wind for the Castile. His passing did not go unnoticed. It was, after all, expected.

Hatless, bloody, and frightened half to death, David Apodaco whipped his horse through the double gates of the mansion. "The townspeople!" he gibbered to the men who ran into the courtyard to see what was going on. "They've gone crazy! They're killing everyone!"

Durán appeared. He was frowning, which was unusual in and of itself, but he never raised his voice as he issued a stream of orders. He didn't believe in shouting. It only sowed disorder. He put fifteen men under Vicente Dominguín, the lugubrious *guerrillero*, and Álarid, the bandmaster. They were thundering away from the great house within five minutes after Apodaca's arrival.

Durán watched them go. Then he turned back and went inside. He wasn't going to let a little insurrection by townspeople interrupt the diversion he had planned for that evening.

Hidden in the trees at the head of the valley, other eyes watched them go too. Doc pulled his watch from his pocket and studied it while Lew Salem struck a match behind his palm. "Give them ten minutes," he said.

Raider nodded and grinned loosely. He was humming to himself. He had sucked up enough of Doc's Egyptian Cure to stun the Stonewall Brigade, and was feeling no pain. Judy licked her lips and gave Doc's hand a quick squeeze in the darkness. David just stared at the big, distant house and clutched his Winchester so hard it seemed he was trying to crush it with his hands.

Ten minutes dragged by interminably. At last Judy, sharper-eyed than Doc and more sober than Raider and so able to read Doc's pocket watch by moonlight, whispered, "It's time."

The party mounted and set off down the valley. There were twenty-one in all: the three Pinks, Lew Salem, David Silver, Judy and fifteen other occupants of Las Peñas. They spread out in a long curving line, with Silver slightly ahead of the rest, setting the pace. They had debated trying to creep in afoot and discarded the notion. It would take too long to cover the distance from the trees to the villa, increasing the chance of discovery. And it would have been too hard to try to keep twenty people coordinated when they were stumbling around in the dark. Instead they opted to come in abreast on horseback, making the best speed they could and counting on the darkness to shield them.

The sound of hoofbeats throbbed in their ears. Doc felt a strange, curdled excitement. He looked at Judy. Her face was drawn, almost skeletal in the darkness. He didn't know what it was, but he knew she had a heavy debt to settle in Henry Durán's fortress.

On his other side rode Raider, swaying dangerously in the saddle. From time to time Doc heard snatches of the low song Rade was singing to himself: "De Camptown

Racers sing this song, doo-da, doo-da—'' He wondered if it had been a good idea to let Raider come. On the other hand, he was a good hand in a fight, and had a stake of his own to settle. Besides, Doc was afraid to try to tell him not to.

They cut the distance to the villa in half, then quartered it. A couple of lanterns glowed on the walls, but the main house was lit up, isolated and splendid, an island of light in a sea of blackness.

On the western wall, Curly Snow paused to share a sip of his bottle with Toby Sublette. Toby's big Sharps was propped against the parapet nearby. He tipped the bottle back and froze. "Hey, don't hog it all," Curly laughed.

Toby threw the bottle over the wall and spat out a mouthful of whiskey. "Sound the alarm," he snapped huskily. "There's riders comin'!" He dove for the rifle.

With Vicente Dominguín at their head, the column of horsemen rode through the mountains for Las Peñas as fast as darkness and the width of the trail would let them.

As they began to pass under the jut of boulders Raider had noticed before, a brawny arm thatched with coarse red hair twisted home a plunger. Twenty sticks of dynamite went off with a roar. Rocks and trees and earth swept down like a tidal wave. Five horses and riders disappeared beneath the avalanche. Vicente Dominguín wouldn't be tying any more of his enemies over maguey shoots, not after three tons of mountainside landed on the dome of his balding head.

Higher up the slope Geordie McCassick climbed to his feet and began shaking one big fist. "Have at ye, ye Sassenach swine!" he shouted at the riders milling below. From a clump of rocks to his right two more of Eloy Martínez's sons began peppering the Thieves with rifle fire, adding to their confusion and demoralization.

A tiny tongue of flame winked suddenly from the wall surrounding the villa of La Castilla. Mark Guthrie, a carpenter, grunted softly and fell from the back of his horse as the low thud of a rifle shot reached the riders' ears. Doc stood up in his stirrups. "Ride!" he yelled. "Ride for all you're worth."

The party broke into a run across the remaining distance. In the blackness it was quite dangerous. Thirty yards to Doc's left a stone turned beneath a horse's hoof, spilling animal and rider.

Another shot boomed from the wall. Lew Salem's mare screamed and went over, Lew barely managing to jump free in time. Doc angled Judith, who had fallen behind the fleeter horses, in his direction as the young editor picked himself up off the ground. He stretched down a hand and pulled Lew up after him. "Much obliged," Salem said. Judith put her ears back but didn't balk. This was far too serious for that.

A hundred yards separated them from the wall. Another rifle shot—fired from the same gun as before, by the sound—and another rider cried out and fell. David Silver hauled in on the reins of his paint and slipped from the saddle. He was sitting on the ground with his rifle at his shoulder as Doc and Lew went lumbering past on Judith.

The young man sighted carefully at the spot where he judged the fire had been coming from. His eyes made out the humped form of a man crouched behind the wall, caught the gleam of torchlight from a gun barrel. He fired.

The bullet took Toby Sublette in the throat. He stood up, blinking his narrow pit bull eyes and trying to swallow, as blood gushed down the front of his shirt. Then he pitched headfirst over the wall.

Other men were firing from the wall. Others were straining to shut the double gates. Whooping, leaning low over the neck of his bay like a jockey, Raider curved around and went streaking in through the main gates with two of the locals just behind.

A shotgun boomed from the door. One of the townsmen was plucked out of his saddle as if by an invisible hand. Raider dropped like a sack of grain to the ground on the far side of his bay as a second shot scythed air above his saddle. "Them's your two," he said cheerily. Lying on his belly he shot Isham Lee twice, between the sidestepping legs of the bay. The black man staggered back and fell across the doorway.

Judy reined her horse in right next to the wall beside the gate. She was wearing jeans now; it wasn't the time for femininity. She tucked her feet up, stood on the saddle, and boosted herself up onto the wall. The surviving townsman was trying to control his wounded horse and throwing shots at a knot of Thieves just inside the gate. Judy shot one through the neck as he drew bead on the local and the others scattered. Judy dropped to the ground, crouched low for a moment to get her bearings. She saw Raider bound across the still form in the doorway and got up to follow him. Her green eyes were cold and purposeful.

All along the western side of the compound men were clambering over the wall, grappling with defenders or blazing away at them. Doc steered for the gates. He and Lew dismounted as David Silver loped up with his rifle in one hand. The three of them put their shoulders to the gates and swung them open.

Figures appeared around the corner of the great house. Lew Salem fired at them and they ducked back. A shot crashed from an upstairs window. A man coming over the wall toppled backwards.

Raider didn't pause when he crossed the threshold, but kept moving, back into the house to the corridor where he'd been kept prisoner. He ran along the hall, peering in the grates. The rooms were dark and empty. He cursed and ran back the way he'd come.

Judy and the local who'd made it in the gate with Raider stepped into the house at the same time. A glittering thing spun out of the doorway to the left and struck the local with a thump. He sank, the hilt of a dagger protruding from his chest.

Judy threw herself to the side and fired. She was sure she'd missed. She ducked down beside the stairs where she could keep an eye on the front, the door from which the knife had come, and the passage to the back of the house.

She saw Doc just outside the door. He had his sawed-off shotgun in his immaculately gloved hands. Rapidly she shook her head. He saw her, nodded, stopped. She gestured at the left-hand doorway with her eyes.

He stepped through, pivoted smartly, and fired both barrels from the hip. Miguelito Díaz swung around from behind the door frame in time to be virtually cut in two at the waist. Doc swung around with his back to the wall and drew his pistol.

Footfalls behind Judy. She wheeled. It was Raider barging back down to the front. "Cells're empty," he yelled. "Upstairs!" And he was by her, taking the stairs two at a time.

He didn't know where either of the Duráns' bedrooms was. He decided to go right, for the hell of it. He heard puffing behind him, turned back to jeer at Doc for getting so out of shape he couldn't even climb stairs without wheezing like a locomotive on a twenty-percent grade.

It wasn't Doc, but middle-aged Luke Robertson with a carbine in his hands. He smiled and nodded to Raider as if they were out hunting rabbits. Motioning him to follow, Raider slipped down the corridor.

Still flying high on laudanum, Raider guessed the bedroom would be at the end of the corridor, where it could get a corner view. He strode toward it with Robertson on his heels.

It happened so fast Raider had no time to think. A door behind and to his left popped open and two shots crashed out. Robertson gasped and fell forward into Raider. He looked into the Pinkerton's face through his glasses, smiled apologetically, and died.

Again, a flicker of motion. Raider threw himself backwards. A bullet splintered wood over his head.

He hadn't so much as gotten a square look at his assailant, but he knew who it was. Of all the Thieves, only Slowhand

McVie was that fast. Much as Raider hated to admit it, the white-blond kid was faster than he.

He scrambled to the last door on the right, jerked it open, and dove inside. A bullet gouged the jamb at his heels. *Jesus, the kid's good.* He glanced around. He was in a darkened bedroom dominated by a huge canopied bed, with a full-length mirror in a revolving frame at the foot of it. Counterpane and hangings were an indigo so deep as to be almost black. This had to be Sancha's room. Obviously Deborah wasn't here. But at the moment the Pink's main concern was making sure he got out of the room alive.

He shut the door quietly. He would have just a few heartbeats before Slowhand came through that door. He was going to need a hell of a dodge to beat the kid's uncanny reflexes.

Doc disappeared through the doorway to the left of the entrance. In a moment David Silver entered with his pistol in hand. A hubbub of voices from the other parts of the house indicated that other invaders were gaining access through windows or other doors.

From above came a spatter of shots. David froze with his boot on the first tread of the stairs. Judy was right behind him, stuffing fresh cartridges into the cylinder of her revolver. Several of the Las Peñans joined them.

From somewhere above came a woman's scream. David went white and lunged up the stairs. The rest followed in a mob.

Walking soft, Slowhand McVie crept down the hall to Sancha Durán's bedroom. He put his gloved hand on the cut-crystal doorknob and smiled. If the damned spy thought he'd found safety by going to ground here, he was wrong— dead wrong.

Smiling a happy smile he threw open the door. There he was, the idiot, standing in plain view right in front of him! Almost disappointed, Slowhand snapped three quick shots into the gunman who stood facing him ten feet away.

The man shattered into a million diamond-bright shards.

Slowhand was still gaping at the crystal explosion of the mirror when Raider, lying at his ease on the bed, shot him through the right eye. "Old age and treachery," he said, "is always gonna overcome youth and skill." He climbed stiffly off the bed and ran into the hallway. The laudanum was beginning to wear off. He didn't know how much longer he could go on.

As Slowhand McVie was stalking his prey, David mounted the top step and raced down the hallway leading to the back of the house, his followers at his heels. Frantically they began flinging open doors.

"There's somebody in—" a thin shop clerk in his thirties began as he peered into a darkened room. A thick blade chunked into the middle of his forehead and his face disappeared in a welter of blood.

Tearing his machete free of his first victim's skull, Marcosio Abadón sprang among the Las Peñans, laying about with the huge knife. Judy saw David Silver go to his knees, blood gouting from his shoulder. Another man fell back clutching the spurting stump of his wrist. The last turned to run, and Abadón took his head off his shoulders in a mighty swipe. Then, not even seeming to see the Pinkerton, the giant turned back and raised his weapon to finish Silver.

"Abadón," she called, her voice soft but full of hate. He paused and turned his mighty head to look at her.

When his eyes found hers she shot him in the belly.

He fell back a step. She shot him again, saw blood blossom against his shirt. He swayed, and started to take a step forward.

Frantically, Judy emptied the gun into his massive chest. The impact of the bullets drove him back, step by step, until at the sixth shot be fell backwards out the tall arched window at the end of the hall. An instant later she heard his body thump on the ground. Her knees gave way beneath her.

Raider almost tripped over her as he came out of the

right-hand corridor. He started to bend down, but she waved him away. She was getting back to her feet as he raced the length of the left-hand hallway.

He wasn't more than halfway there before the door at the end burst open. Sancha Durán stood there, stark naked, flushed at her cheeks and belly, her nipples in full erection. "Stand back!" she shrieked. "You can't have her."

He stopped. He knew he should have killed her, but somehow he couldn't bring himself to shoot her in cold blood, no matter what she was. "I killed him," she panted. "He wouldn't let me have her. So I killed him!"

Raider frowned. "Who?"

"*My brother!*" Sancha screamed. She snatched a kerosene lantern from its bracket on the wall and smashed it to the floor between them. Flames soared up with a ravenous roar.

The madwoman ran back into the room. Raider held his arms up before his face, muttered a prayer, and leapt. He could smell burning hide and hair when he came out of the flames, but he was unharmed.

He wouldn't stay that way for long if he couldn't get out of there pronto. He was cut off now by the wall of fire. He plunged into the room.

Deborah Silver lay on her back, stark naked, with her wrists bound to the head rail of a big brass bed, and her feet tied spread wide to the bottom posts. Her eyes were big and round with terror.

Henry Durán lay on his stomach next to her. He wore a purple silk dressing gown trimmed in yellow. The back of it was somewhat discolored by the blood that had spread from the single-bit ax buried between his shoulder blades. His face was turned toward the captive girl, but his yellow eyes were not taking in her beauty.

Sancha Durán threw herself on the bed and clung to Deborah. "She's mine," she said, half snarling. "Henry wanted her, but she was mine. You want her, but I'll burn her first. We'll all burn!"

Raider's hand was beginning to shake with fatigue and

reaction. He didn't dare try shooting Sancha for fear of hitting Deborah. He stepped forward. "There, now, Sancha," he said. "Don't you want me in bed with you too? Ain't it more fun that way?"

She eyed him with a glare as hot and yellow as the flames that crackled at his back. "Stay away!"

He took another step. She sprang up and grabbed the lamp above the bed and threw it right at his face. He just managed to deflect it with his hand. It shattered against the wall, smearing flames in a broad swath.

Raider lunged for the bed. He struck Sancha with his shoulder, knocking her sprawling away, and came down across Deborah. He seized the ax haft one-handed and ripped it free of Henry Durán's back. Hauling himself up he began to hack at the ropes holding Deborah's wrists.

The bedclothes nearest the door were beginning to smolder. The ropes parted. Deborah tried to sit up, rubbing her wrists to restore circulation. Raider turned to cut at the ropes that bound her feet. Sancha jumped on him.

He threw her off onto the floor. A wild swipe severed the rope at Deborah's right ankle, but a bright line of blood appeared where he had nicked her flesh. He hesitated. Sancha threw herself at him again, grappling him with incredible strength. Her fingers clawed for his eyes.

His Remington lay on the bed. Deborah picked it up by the barrel and hit Sancha in the face with it. The raven-haired woman squalled like a cat. Raider heaved her off and struck her in the shoulder with the blunt side of the axhead. She reeled back against a huge, ancient wardrobe and fell.

Half the room was ablaze. In the light of the fire and the sole surviving lantern Raider took careful aim and chopped through the final rope. He hauled Deborah off the bed with one arm and with the other threw the ax through the window.

"Hey down there!" he shouted. The courtyard seemed to spin beneath him. Faces were turned up, fingers pointing at the flame-lit window. Friend or enemy? With an almost shattering surge of relief he recognized Lew Salem's long face.

The fire was getting uncomfortably near. "Go on," he told Deborah. She paused a moment, then climbed out the window and let herself hang while Raider kept a grip on her wrist. Lew caught her by the ankles, and then Doc was there, and several others, taking hold of the girl and easing her to the dirt.

With a wild scream Sancha Durán threw the last lamp. It exploded practically between Raider's feet. He screamed as the flames seared his legs and back. His clothes afire, he jumped onto the windowsill and then launched himself in a long leap. He struck and went down hard, rolling over and over to douse the flames that ate at his hair and skin.

He heard Sancha's voice rising shrill into the night as the flames had their way with her. And he would never know if she was screaming—

Or laughing.

CHAPTER FIFTEEN

Creaking and groaning, the AOA wagon made its way up the long grade west out of Las Peñas, heading for Las Vegas, the A.T.&S.F. railhead, and, eventually, St. Louis. Doc sat on the box, smoking a cheroot, his derby tipped to one side, Judy sitting next to him looking altogether cool and lovely in her Gypsy blouse and skirt.

Raider rode alongside. He looked a little funny, with his head wrapped in bandages like a turban. But Doc reckoned all the hair on his head would grow back in time, as would the skin of his back, so he didn't see why Raider was wearing such a sour expression.

It may have been because everything hadn't turned out quite the way they might have wished, back in Las Peñas. Instead of being unceremoniously dumped, Mayor Stone and Police Chief Broward were at this very moment appearing before the territorial legislature in Santa Fe, busily claiming every smidgen bit of credit for busting up the Forty Thieves. In the meantime, the peace of Las Peñas had been placed in the capable hands of Broward's two new assistants, Grant Largo and Larkin "Preacher" Hanks.

"Nothin's ever been proved against these men," Broward told Doc and Raider the day he left for Santa Fe. "The whole matter of the Forty Thieves is still under investigation. And you can't deny, these here boys is mighty capable."

Well, no, you couldn't.

The other Thieves were dead, fled, or imprisoned. The

only survivor of the perpetrators of the roadhouse massacre was Claude Baker, whom Officers Largo and Hanks, among others, were only to eager to discharge their civic duties by testifying against. It looked as if the stubby dynamiter was going to spend the next million years or so in the pen. Other than that . . . it looked as if the townspeople who had taken part in the final battle were not going to be persecuted. Stone and Broward swore up and down nothing would be done to them for "taking the law into their own hands." Doc was just as glad he'd had the men who took out the Thieves in Las Peñas wear masks.

Or maybe Raider was looking sour because his prized mustache had come through the wars resembling an old, singed toothbrush.

Not everything they left behind was bad. David Silver's collarbone was knitting nicely. And while Doc felt a definite pang every time he thought of lovely dark-haired Deborah, he had seen definitely lingering looks passing between her and Lew Salem that night at the Castile. *Ah, well,* he thought. *I suppose it's better that way.*

Judy was chewing pensively on a stalk of timothy. "I wonder," she said, "if—"

"—if they're ever going to find Abadón's body," Doc filled in. He sighed and shook his head. "It must have been consumed in the fire. It surely wasn't going to get very far, was it?"

She gazed at him, green eyes wide. He thought again how beautiful she was, and dutifully thrust the thought from his mind. His experience with Deborah had taught him his lesson; he was through with women. This week, anyway.

"Come now," he said sternly. "You don't think, with six bullets in him, after falling fifteen feet, you don't think there's any possible way he could have *survived*."

She looked away. "I guess not."

"Of course not." He settled back in the box.

He felt her hand at the back of his neck, stroking his

hair. It gave him an unsettling feeling of déjà vu. He turned to her. "What are you doing that for?" he demanded.

She eyed him for a moment and tossed away the timothy stem. "Because I like to." She kissed him.

He returned the kiss briefly, then broke off. "What's going on here?"

"Nothing much," Judy Holiday said, "except that I've been falling in love with you since the moment I met you."

Doc nodded absently. "I see. That explains—you *what?*" He goggled at her.

She started to unfasten his tie. "You heard me."

"I—uh—well—yes." Her fingers started on the buttons of his shirt. "My word! Not out here where everybody can *see!*"

She wrapped her arms around him and kicked backwards off the footboard. They fell into the wagon together in a heap on a pile of baggage. Giggling like adolescents, they began to disengage one another from their clothes.

Judith cocked her big ears briefly backwards. They perked up when she was satisfied she knew what was going on. She hated it when Doc drove; he seemed to have the notion he knew more about being a mule than she did, and was always interfering.

His bay having fallen back a little ways, Raider came trotting up alongside the AOA wagon. He did a take when he saw Judith plodding along with no one in the box. For a moment he stared at the wagon. Laughter wasn't coming from inside anymore. It had been replaced by a rhythmic thumping, interspersed with low, heartfelt moans.

"Well I," Raider announced, "will be dipped in shit and fried for a hush puppy."

No one answered except the birds scolding each other through the trees. Raider rode alongside in increasingly sullen silence for a few minutes, listening to the sounds coming from the wagon.

A thought struck him. He began to smile beneath his

ruined mustache. *Let them lovebirds have their fun*, he thought. *I got some fish of my own to fry.*

He swung the bay's head back around the way they'd come. As the road curved back around into sight of the village, he booted the horse on to a trot, then a lope.

Then he said, "The hell with it," and lined out at a dead run for Las Peñas, and a certain tavern run by a certain redheaded tavern-keeper.

JAKE LOGAN